HOW THE MOON WORKS

[STORIES]

MATT ROWAN

Copyright © 2021

Print ISBN: 978-1-941462-24-9
eBook ISBN: 978-1-941462-23-2

Cover and book design by Andrew Keating.

Cobalt Press
Denver, CO

cobaltreview.com

For all inquiries, including requests for review materials, please contact cobalt@cobaltreview.com.

For Joyce Derwin, one of the kindest people I've ever had the privilege to call a friend

contents

how the moon works

no me
say it

What majesty, what joy, what colors, what pangloss, said the
announcers as they opened to Handle-Hands' segment. It filled
your mind's eye with images of 1980s soap opera intros and the
loving visage of famous-but-not-too-famous soap celebrity Ray
MacDonnell, big eyebrowed and winsome grinning. Handle-
Hands, himself, had something about the very same Ray
MacDonnell to his facial appearance, and he induced nostalgia
with his winsomeness when he grinned into the wand-like
microphone they fixed in place to one of his appendages.
People reported being stirred to reminisce mid-viewing and
then feeling transported back to the summer cottages of their

youth, swimming in adjacent pond and roasting marshmallows in the open air, as though both experiences were happening simultaneously while also viewing.

Handle-Hands eventually became accustomed to his celebrity on Home Shopping Network's *Welcome to Products That Will Scare You.* His role was "horrifying host."

People liked to laugh at how Handle-Hands struggled to hold things, specifically products of many shapes and many sizes. Everyone was always grabbing Handle-Hands' hands, which were handles, and telling him that he was the doorway to their heart. They explained that his manner, in addition to something else they couldn't *quite* place, made him their favorite salesman of all time, on TV or anywhere. He never knew how to respond.

His handles were two different kinds of knobs, one brass and the other crystal. They weren't like hooks or something on a pirate. They weren't foreign. They were part of his body. He'd feel it if they got hurt. He felt it when people turned them, especially the overzealous people who turned them much harder than was ever required. You could see him wince, and in that wince he seemed to call upon a much larger segment of kinder-gentler humanity to magically will itself into existence. And oh how the imbeciles would struggle, gurgling a bit and then sneering at his handle hands, which were knobs, and grabbing them more vigorously and turning them more vigorously, sometimes honking as they did so, too.

"It's a real pleasure, Mr. Handle-Hands—an honor! Honor is all mine!!" they'd say, grinding their molars during the struggle with his knobs, never noticing how their human hands were agonizing poor Handle-Hands. He was polite and never mentioned the agony they put him through. It was unclear, really, why the people would grab him so vigorously, feel such a need to turn his handles with such ferocity. He was not a door and turning harder would no sooner open him up to them, but they turned all the harder, as society had seemingly trained them to do.

What horror would visit the man who hosted *Welcome to Products That Will Scare You* in consistent waves of fan fervor.

His hosting duties mainly entailed attempting to juggle whatever product was being sold at that particular moment in TV time. He was supposed to fail. The products were supposed to fall, but the products could not be shown breaking, if they did break. So they always shot Handle-hands from the above the waist. "Ta-da!" someone would say, while the broadcast displayed an unbroken, previously recorded image of the product.

He knew why he did it. One reason was the obvious need for money. Another was the not-obvious fascination he had with some form of renown—even if minor, as this most certainly was minor. The third and most important reason was for his bundle at home, with her own tiny knobs, which were very different from his own, both white. He worried about what would happen as she got older, and perhaps recognizable to viewers. Would her knobs be as wrenched and turned mercilessly as his were, all too often?

He fought desperately to keep her a secret—came home, met with the nanny, changed her diaper, fed her dinner, polished her knobs. Her porcelain knobs. In every characteristic of beauty, she was superior to him. And so precious, so fragile! He could not forget how fragile she was. He was as careful carrying her as he'd ever been with anything, carrying her like his own existence somehow would be snuffed out if ever he loosened his hold. The sun squelched, the universe emptied into oblivion.

He vowed to protect every part of her. While he was still living and breathing and able to cradle her in his handled arms, no one would ever grip her away from him.

Then came the introduction of one particular Product That Will Scare You: the No Me Say It.

❄

The No Me Say It was introduced to the buying public on a rainy Saturday. The whole country was simultaneously experiencing rain. It was great for sales. People were in front of their televisions looking for things to buy, especially things that scared them. If it actually harmed them, all the better.

The No Me Say It was sandwiched between two other products that Handle-Hands' bosses had higher opinions of going into the day's selling. The first was an object that looked a lot like a soccer ball and was about the same size but with electrical sockets inside of which you plugged metal rods, and you plugged its cord into a household electric socket—rubber gloves for fitting metal rods into plugs that were not included. The Shocker Jockey. Things that forced an electric current through people always sold well.

The second was a Build-Your-Own Troll that came to life after you finished constructing it, and, alive, would attempt to singe you with its singe-stick. Then, once singed, the troll would cut you, cut you a lot. Cut you where it hurts. It would cut you with a machine called "The Paper-Cut Machine." Included with the purchase of a Build-Your-Own Troll.

By comparison, the No Me Say It was unremarkable, and that's what made it so remarkable.

When Handle-Hands had first got his start in the business of home shopping, he had a mentor, Robes Johannasen, whose one crucial piece of advice had remained with Handle-Hands all these years: "One day, from what reaches, depths, what have you, will come a thing that sells better than all the things you've ever sold. That thing has a life of its own. Don't get in the way of that thing or it just might be the end of you. It might even suck you dry."

Robes' *thing* was an expensive electronic leech measuring three feet in length, about one in width. He had a very straightforward sense of the world. Few corpses were so desiccated as his when they found him dead on his dressing-room floor.

The No Me Say It surprised Handle-Hands. He didn't really think much about the small and strange device, until he was forced to, because of its meteoric success. People stopped him on the streets about the No Me Say It, saying they thought it was just junk, but then it saved their lives with terror, the skillful implementation of slow-dripping, methodical terror. They didn't even bother to grab Handle-Hands' knobs anymore. His knobs were so clean, so unblemished and germ-free, even after a long day's work and being out in the world as a recognizable television person. The experience was brand new to him, not that he minded.

But the No Me Say It, it wouldn't let him sleep.

The device was simple. Whenever you tried to say anything, it would caw, via its speakers: "NO, *ME SAY IT!*" As time went on, and you continued your ownership of it, the noise would get progressively louder. And that might be fine, if it ever stopped getting louder. It made your eyes bleed, after a short while. After a short while it would react to every noise you made, every breath, every swallow, every snore and snort, whether superfluous or necessary.

And even if you were able to rest, your rest was restless. The No Me Say It appeared in your dreams like a winged serpent, a screeching horror on the worst side of a succubus. And even if you were able to rest the rest of the restless, your eyes still bled from the noise, bled closed.

It was a massive hit. You couldn't listen to the radio without hearing the cacophony of the No Me Say It, mainly because your own No Me Say It would exceed the sound of the music, overwhelming the volume of any music or ambiance or whatever else was producing sound, naturally. A few satisfied customers' heads exploded. In actual fact. Their heads blew up. So too did melons. The produce section of a busy grocery store was one of the worst places to have your No Me Say It. Fresh, ripened melon, unexploded, began fetching a hefty price.

People loved that the No Me Say It had the power to follow you everywhere, whether you wanted it to or not.

And they all realized quite abruptly it was Handle-Hands who was to thank. They raced to Handle-Hands like a horde of hard-charging, single-minded livestock. Now, rather than be ignored and kept safe from further harm by people's infatuation with a particular product he'd sold, Handle-Hands was their singular object of worship. He had given them the No Me Say It. He had given them something so clearly apart from want, so clearly and in every way the embodiment of need. The need for something so terribly true.

Handle-Hands was soon overwhelmed by the abusive praise. He fled. He remembered Johannasen's other words, "There's nothing doing so why try? Let them. Fierce shouts. Don't. The rubber pillow. I'm just trying to be understood." It was important to note that these were words Johannasen had said very near the end, when his total blood loss was near its apex. Something about his words, though, made Handle-Hands think of his daughter. She had never been gifted a No Me Say It. He hoped she'd be able to sleep well without it, but there was Handle-Hands's own No Me Say It to consider, the noise of which was enough to keep everyone in a single household awake for the entirety of their lives.

He felt the weariness of his body closing in, the lack of sleep suffocating him—delirious, but aware enough of what was truly important.

The horde caught up to him on Culver Drive, but he'd lost them again by the time he got to his neighborhood and the street he lived on. He worried they'd be waiting for him there. He was surprised that his adoring fans, whose effusive "thank yous" were only exceeded in decibel by the sound of the peoples' No Me Say Its, were not teeming to greet him. It was possible they were hiding, but the No Me Say It made hiding difficult, if not completely impossible. There was only the sound of his own No Me Say It shouting over his most necessary and automatic bodily functions, a slow trickle of blood down his face.

Inside his home, Handle-Hands noticed immediately how much cooler the temperature was. The world had been something like superheated by the increased noise. It was spreading its ubiquity to other sensations. It might have been stimulating an end to all things, but probably strictly an end to all comfort. Life would go on, irritably.

For now, at least it was cool and quiet in Handle-Hands's home. He went up the stairs to Missy's room. There she was, resting. She had slept! Her nanny was nearby, seated on a rocking chair, reading. She signaled to him: Handle-Hands. *Quiet. Let her sleep. Let her enjoy this little comfort while it lasts.* The nanny looked profoundly uncomfortable.

Handle-Hands backed quietly from his daughter's room.

The sun, previously shining into the living room, was now blotted out. And there was a tremor, a tremble, slight at first, but increasing in intensity. There was a hill some football fields from Handle-Hands's neighborhood. On that hill had risen a statue. It was his own likeness. It was Handle-Hands. There was the teeming mass of adulating fans. On the hill. They'd hauled the enormous statue of Handle-Hands up the hill. The noise was deafening. They must have waited for him to go inside his home. They'd had to have been collectively holding their breath with fierce patience and at some personal risk, waiting for the right moment to raise the statue and begin their applause. And while they were now doing precisely that, No Me Say Its were drowning out the noise of their applause. His own No Me Say It had sounded. So had the nanny's. Missy was crying out, awoken, stricken from comfort. This infuriated Handle-Hands. How infuriating! He forced his No Me Say It from his pocket with the nubs of his handles, let it fall to the floor. He began to trample it with his feet. It would not break, not this high-quality product. Not so easily. He knocked over other items previously showcased on *Welcome to Products That Will Scare You*: the Mouth Television, a television that would try to gum on you—*it didn't have teeth!*—when you weren't watching it, and sometimes when you were, if you weren't giving the watching your all, and sometimes when you were giving it your all, because it was a product that kept its users on their toes; the Dear Head of a Deer, which floated after you disembodied, trying to gore with its sword antlers, because it had sword blades that were bent and shaped like jagged antlers for antlers; the Wearing a Glass Necklace, which would get progressively tighter and sharper over the course of a good, fun night out on the town; The Bat, which was both a baseball bat and an animal bat and would flutter its wings every time you swung it at something, simultaneously putting you at the risk of acquiring rabies and hitting dingers. Lots of other items, too, all of which broke easily. But his No Me Say It did not, as though it were refusing, as it shouted "*NO, ME SAY IT!*" amid the destruction.

And while Handle-Hands's living room shook from his anger and desperation, the ground outside likewise continued to shake from the noise of the people and the noise of their No Me Say Its. They'd become so voracious, lost in their fandom, panicking with elation. They wouldn't mean to, but they might soon inadvertently destroy something beautiful in their haste and the scrum to press themselves against their favorite TV celebrity.

It didn't come to pass quite that way, though. The statue was not secured in its position, and so a blast of wing tipped the visage of Handle-Hands, both of his knobs raised in triumph to the sky. Now falling, falling and so felled. The earth cracked. A sinkhole? Or maybe nothing was ever beneath the earth's surface and it had only been presumed, taken it on faith, that geologists were being honest, leading us to believe we existed on largely solid ground. Regardless, a caving occurred and the statue and some of Handle-Hands many admirers perished into the widening cavity, echoes of screaming and No Me Say Its gradually fading into the vast depth of their plunge.

And while this sinkhole or void to another dimension or the emptiness of the earth spread farther and farther outside, it simultaneously pulled apart the interior of Handle-Hands's home. His home was torn, halved, made a duplex not very dexterously. Handle-Hands, aware of this development, left his No Me Say It, which did indeed disappear forever then, into the void. He scrambled up his stairs to Missy's bedroom, where the nanny had been comforting her and had now wrapped missy up against the far wall on the opposite side of the room, attempting to shield and protect her. The floor in the completely halved room aimed downward at its break. Furniture and rugs and all other items that had previously inhabited the room so benignly were sliding, tumbling and gone. "Handle-Hands," shouted the nanny. "Ren!" shouted Handle-Hands, remembering his nanny had a name and that her name was *Ren* and that now, not only did he worry for his daughter's safety, but for hers as well, for Ren's, as though she too were family, because, now that he thought about it, she *was* family.

The floor was smooth hardwood, heretofore covered in many throw rugs. There was very little to catch one's footing on, especially as the floor's decline grew sharper. Handle-Hands had anchored his arm around a protruding crack in the floorboards at the house's furthest edge. He dangled there. "Try jumping to me, Ren," he said. "Grab my handle!" He waved his free arm and the knob attached. But just as he shouted to her, Ren finally lost her own footing and began to roll toward the cavity, and so too did Missy, wailing as she went. But Ren, wits about her or operating on some kind of maternal instinct and adrenaline pumping, reached out for the pearl knob of Missy, taking it, and in a rush, compelled herself to the awaiting knob of Handle-Hands, taking hold of it, too, caught between the two of them, immediately straining to maintain her hold on each.

These were the typical challenges of *life-or-death-in-the-balance* situations: Handle-Hands pulling with every ounce of his bodily might, as was Ren. But it was no use. They couldn't lift themselves out of their precarious spot. They might have let themselves go in only another minute or two, so bleak was the situation. Handle-Hands prayed for a *deus ex machina* to come and save him—no, not him—Missy, Ren, spare them this fate. But it didn't come, or it did but not as he expected it would.

It didn't come from above. It came from the one place he hadn't expected. It came from his daughter. She opened her mouth, and all the tumult and calamity around them was sucked up into her. She possessed the nascent power to make bad things disappear, or so was becoming apparent. The destruction was sucked up into her, a vacuum very different from the one that had been building around them. And once the trembling had stopped, the scariness of the situation seemed to lift, too. Ren and Handle-Hands pulled Missy and themselves from the tenuously stable but still completely destroyed room. They escaped the house, which tilting, was finally freed of its foundation and collapsed into the hole. But they were still there. They were on solid ground. Things felt all right.

Things felt really good.

They—the three of them—decided to lie down in the grass of a neighbor's lawn and rejoice, despite all that had happened. Emergency responders told them that they were in a state of shock.

If that is the worst of it, Handle-Hands thought, *then let it be.*

grizzly 25's

There was hair, a lot of it, but more notable were the searing red eyes—eyes that watched carefully and closely. A scarred face from so many years out in the thicket, the thick-of-it, what this was. So many lights. But those no longer bothered it, not very much. It could see clearly. The weight of the thing that it was— 1650 lbs or so. It still moved swiftly.

The boy. He wandered around because he was told to, by his folks. "Have fun, Son. Good luck. We know you can do this."

Their tears, though. The boy didn't feel confident. The employee, the one with the scraggly beard, gave him the OK to pass beyond the velvet rope. The boy was scared, sure. He didn't know why he was there. The narrow, winding pathway he now trod down was marked by strange aggregations of old arcade games, most of which were powered down, and some of them had deep claw marks embedded in their control panels or on the garish illustrations etched along the cabinets' sides.

The boy rounded a corner, found real bones littering the tiled floor. He knelt to study the bones, to be sure he was not letting his imagination take his mind over. He was mature for his age in that way. The bones were real, very real, real as any he'd ever seen before. The bones were child-sized. They'd been gnawed on pretty good, a few broken in half. That was all it took for panic to set in, for him to let instinct take control.

He turned to run, but there it was.

He let out a yell, but the bear was already upon him.

Grizzly 25's Pizza & Par-Tee Zone. Sheila had longed to get away just as soon as she could. Life had been a semi-organized rut since she was a teenager, when Dad left Mom and Mom left Dad on the exact same day. They both left notes. Sheila found the notes in different parts of their home. Mom's was on the coffee table in front of the TV and Dad's was in the bathroom taped above the toilet, hanging like it ought to be a photo of the whole family together during happier times. Both of her parents regretted leaving Sheila behind, they said in their respective notes. Both parents said they could no longer stand the sight of the other. Each stated that it was for that reason they had to go and be gone for good, to insure they'd never see the other again. Each figured by taking Sheila with them, they'd create the very likely possibility of seeing the other again, and that was a possibility neither had it in them to accept. Each truly hated the other.

Sheila was eighteen and had nearly graduated high school by the time the authorities finally got wind of her situation. And *graduation* being a loose term for what she was about to do, since her grades had suffered mightily due to the extra energy she'd expended each day pretending her family still existed. She was a sharp kid. She managed to pass a lot of classes by the skin of her teeth. She completed the remaining credits required to graduate over the summer following her senior year. Sheila got work at Grizzly 25's that far back, during high school. She was twenty-seven now.

She couldn't believe what she'd seen. Years and years of kids slaughtered wasn't the half of it. Her only friend—one of the few, at least, and the only one among her coworkers—was Dannie. Lots of her coworkers liked her, but, other than Dannie, most of them creeped her out. They bore the weight of their work a little too serenely and it showed. Talked up its benefit to society. Especially Dale. Dale was the worst of the co-workers. Dale was *creepy*.

Dannie told her Dale was more than he seemed, but Sheila couldn't believe it. He was less. He was much less. Still, she had to admit that she didn't know him terribly well, and she based her opinion mostly on how much Dale would laugh about everything, all the time. Sheila had trouble laughing. She couldn't do it at work. She hated laughing there. It was hard enough to fake a smile.

"That may be, honestly, but I mean, there's a rumor circulating that *he's* Grizzly 25," Dannie said. "See where I'm going with this?"

"No, I don't see how he could be a bear."

"Of course I've never seen it, either, but I've heard things about what the bear's like up close. There's a reason they keep it out of view of the public, inside the Grizzly Maze, and not just because of the horrible spectacle of violence. The bear's animatronic. Just like any of these places used to be. Except, instead of playing in a backwood-style country band, the bear eats the kids or maims them horribly till they're dead or close."

Dannie was smoking where she shouldn't have been. Ms. Wunderlee was going to pulverize her if she'd found her there. That was all Sheila could think: how much trouble Dannie'd be in if Ms. Wunderlee caught her. Dannie flicked the cigarette, crushed it under the ball of her left foot, and fanned away the residual smoke, which didn't get rid of the smell but appeared to be a necessary maneuver, nonetheless.

"You're too casual about all this," Sheila said, scowling and then looking down, unable to meet Dannie at eye level.

Dannie seized on Sheila's accusation, "What about the kids? What else can we do? We didn't make this place. We'd probably, neither of us, work here, if we didn't have to, if we're being honest. But we do. I don't like it. Not at all. But it's here or nowhere or someplace else—someplace that could be worse for all I know. Hard to imagine, but not impossible. Have you tried to get a job in another place? Do you even know what other jobs there are?"

"No, I was talking about your smoking. You can't do that in here. If you were gone, well, I don't know. So you have to stay."

"Yeah, well, I don't think Ms. Wunderlee's still here anyway. The kitchen staff wouldn't be talking about stealing a garbage bag full of leftover pizza if she was. There's gonna be some sort of get together after work, ok. Please, say you'll go?"

"Oh c'mon, Dannie. Fine, fine. But will you stop smoking in here? No more. Do it outside."

"Yes, ok, this'll be great. You are going to have a little bit of fun for once," Dannie said. "It's my mission in life to ensure Sheila Franks has some fun before she dies."

Dannie was already on her way. Sheila wished she could have found it in her to say no, but Dannie brought out a side of Sheila she didn't think existed. Sheila thought sometimes Dannie might have been who she herself could have been, had she had a normal adolescence, parents to rebel against. If certain things had worked out differently. If she weren't an employee of Grizzly 25's, with her few middling raises and not a single opportunity for promotion over the past decade. And she should be grateful. That was what wasn't said. She ought to be grateful.

Promoted to what, though, she thought. Some stupid manager? Like Rory? She didn't want to be the kind of person who had to worship at Ms. Wunderlee's altar. Ms. Wunderlee knew how to sting her. That fucking nickname.

The Waif.

The pretend pitying way she'd say it.

Pretend pity. That's why she never told anyone about her situation and scolded herself whenever she accidentally let the details of her situation slip. She always learned the same thing about people: the one way they wanted to experience every aspect of their lives was however was most flattering. They wanted to believe they were good, hence the pity, and they wanted to have fun at others' expense, hence why it was faux pity. She scolded herself for agreeing to go this after-work party thing. Lots of opportunity for pretend pity. She was scolding herself more and more each passing day, it felt like.

*

"I love that you think the grizzly's animatronic, Dannie," Dale was saying to Dannie and a group of coworkers, firelight making his features more devious and therefore having the effect of placing everything he said squarely in doubt. "But no, it's not me. I'm pretty sure it's an actual bear. I'm not willing to test your theory and find out, though."

"I'm not lying," he added.

Sheila had just arrived. She sat quietly. She wanted to sit quietly out of notice for as long as she possibly could. Dannie smiled at her, but that was it for a greeting from her coworkers. A few of them might have nodded, she couldn't be sure. At least no one had called her that name.

"Then where do you go all day?" Dannie pressed him. "You're nowhere in sight for huge lengths of time."

"How would you know?" Dale said.

"My job is to pay attention. I'm the one who makes sure the bear doesn't get loose in the first place," Dannie said. It was true. She sat up in a monitoring tower designed to make certain, and assure worried parents, the grizzly could never escape the Maze. "Just because *you* can't see me, it doesn't mean I'm not there. Kind of like God in that way."

Dale crouched down and made a big show of mockingly kowtowing at Dannie's feet. Dannie rolled her eyes at him and looked away, smirking.

"What happened, you know? Didn't it used to be parents always looked out for their kids, put themselves in harm's way just to prevent kids from getting hurt?" the quiet teenaged-girl who worked in the kitchen, making pizzas and things, said. The others almost didn't hear her. Sheila had strained to listen and felt compelled to respond.

"What do you mean?" Sheila, still not really enjoying herself at all, said.

The teenaged girl who worked in the kitchen looked uncomfortable, but with some visible effort managed to elaborate,"I mean, parents by nature are supposed to be protectors of their young. But then the Par-Tee Zones sprang up and the whole rite of passage was born, an industry based on it. Now kids are left to take one for their parents. Their parents never had to face a gigantic real-life grizzly and survive. But those parents convince themselves that they've had hard lives, too. And they have. Their lives were hard, probably continue to be, but there weren't grizzlies to contend with, not for most people, not usually. And they pretend that all that separates themselves from the grizzly is that velvet rope, like it could come for them, too. But Dannie knows that's an illusion. The bear can't get out of the Grizzly Maze."

The bear couldn't get out of its maze. There was no question about that. Too many safeguards. It didn't matter if the bear was real or fake, it wasn't going to leave the containment zone.

The containment zone, and the Grizzly Maze therein, was a marvel of human ingenuity all its own. It looked a bit haphazardly constructed, given the sheer number of old video games, pinball machines, air hockey tables, arcade basketball units and so forth that were stacked carefully, though precariously seeming, on top of one another (there were steel support beams that skewered the various games and kept them firmly in place).

It was like something out of *A Nightmare on Elm Street*, and this was done entirely on purpose. Children were supposed to feel disoriented in The Maze. It made it easier for the grizzlies to get to them quickly, which was the point: a quick and relatively painful demise for the children unlucky enough to fail to escape The Maze, its long corridors, its many dead-ends. It was very literally a maze. But of course, it was man-made and there were all sorts of security systems in place to prevent the grizzly or grizzlies from escaping, not least of which was the rumored implant that the grizzly had in its brain, which could be detonated by management if nothing else worked.

Parents were supposed to protect their children, they all agreed.

When had the Par-Tee Zone phenomenon started? None of them had had to go through it, but only just barely. Many of them had lost cousins or younger siblings in the Par-Tee Zones. How long ago? Must have been over ten, twenty years, but now it was as if they had always been and always would be.

"They say the whole thing is rigged, that that's why the bear's human. Why else would it be that the kids who always survive are rich brats?" the scraggly bearded employee said, the other one of them who worked in the kitchen. He stubbed out a cigarette and tossed the butt. "It's because of the mom and pop's money. The more things change they stay the same, I'm telling you."

"Yeah, yeah, quit bogarting the pizza. Pass that bag over here," Dale said. The bag was somewhat heavy and full of pizza still, skidding against the hard surface of the ground as it was pulled from one person to the next. And each in their turn took a couple slices.

❋

Sheila was restless in bed that night, tossing and turning before finally drifting into an equally agitated unconscious state. Dreams of her family, those fleeting glimpses of the parents she'd once had, invaded her REM sleep. When she awoke, she knew so much of what she'd dreamed couldn't possibly have happened, wasn't drawn from her actual life. Her father was never so together as he'd been in her dream, never so sober. Her mother never so stable and congenial.

Her father had walked into the kitchen. She couldn't remember if they ever had a normal family breakfast, but in this dream they did. "Good morning to you all," her father said, seeming to dance inside the room, as though floating on air. The dream wasn't a retelling of her early life to the tune of *Leave it to Beaver*. There were subtle moments when the discomfort and unrest that existed between her mother and father appeared, notice-ably. The, "Mornin', Bitch" her father would grumble, at being met by his wife's icy stare. She, in turn, would tell him he could sit wherever a huge pile of shit likes to unload itself, and the silence would resume.

Maybe that's all it had been, the cause of their marriage's disin-tegration, those casual and bitingly sardonic insults that both her parents had let slip in otherwise normal conversation.

Her dream father sat and read the paper, which she really didn't think he ever actually did. MORE PEOPLE THAN EVER PREPARED TO KILL EACH OTHER was a frontpage head-line. Vague statements like that mottled what she could read. YOU'RE SICK BUT PROBABLY NOT DYING; HERE'S HOW TO KNOW FOR SURE.

That was another odd thing about her dream, her dreams as a whole. It's said that our brains can't process written language while we sleep—the part of the brain that interprets the writ-ten word shuts off—but that had never been Sheila's experience. She could read things while dreaming, at least she thought she could. She realized it might just be her brain somehow filling in the blanks, plugging in what it wanted her to read and she was not reading in any serious or deliberate way. Abstract read-ing, as though she could understand a person speaking a for-eign language. But still. Still, in some sense she read while she dreamed, and that was an accomplishment worth noting. She was proud of herself.

In her dream, her father wasn't violent; he was just a dick. Not to her. That remained true. It was just this feeling of a slow and entropic collapse, this general severance of a husband from a wife and a wife from a husband.

Her mother broke a rolling pin, though she'd never been violent in any memorable way either. Why she'd been using a rolling pin at breakfast time, Sheila couldn't imagine. She thought it might have been a tool her mother used to make pancakes in the dream. She rolled them out as though they were pizzas. And then the whole family ate them raw, with only powdered sugar. She remembered there was no butter or syrup. For some reason her mother refused to fry the pancakes in a pan.

"Woman, why do you love me so bad it smells?" her father remarked. In the dream, she wondered if he was drunk. Awake, later, she regretted this thought.

The rolling pin broke against the backside of her father's skull and out flew confetti, as though nothing but party times were happening. But the confetti was like those breath freshener strips that dissolve on your tongue, they were blood red, they became puddles. Scattered across the room melted bloody puddles of confetti. They ruined the pancakes. They ruined everything. And both of her parents turned to her and said, "We'll never leave you, dear. Never."

That's when Sheila woke up.

❋

The following work day, Sheila was standing behind the desk at the prize counter. A child was taking a long time to choose what he wanted. This was typical. His mother encouraged him to pick the army men. He liked army men. "Nah," the boy said, "I have a lot of those."

The line was growing longer and increasingly agitated. Encouragement came first, but that soon gave way to less desirable commentary. "Don't take your time in the Grizzly Maze, little man," the adults said. And then, "This one has had it. You have to shit and get off the pot a lot faster than that if you want to make it through."

The mother turned back and scowled: "You make me sick. Give him a minute. Give him one single minute. He gets his toy, just like all the rest of them. They all get toys when they win something. They all win something!" She began sobbing. Sheila pressed the button that deployed Rory, who was, yes, manager of the Par-Tee Zone, but probably more importantly he was the onsite counselor specializing in grief inhibition. All Par-Tee Zones were required to have a certified grief-inhibitor on staff.

The mother was brought to a chair in the counseling circle. Before attending to her, Rory told Sheila it was going to be a busy day. "This is the sixth incident I've had to respond to already. Our biggest parties haven't arrived yet." He was a worried-looking man. Sheila believed this worked to his advantage when counseling. He certainly always appeared to care and respect the feelings of the patrons he counseled down from whatever shock or misery was visiting them. Sheila both liked and hated that about Rory. She couldn't decide if he was a good person, but she was beginning to wonder, more and more, whether such a person existed anywhere.

She watched Rory attempt to counsel the woman through what was already a traumatic experience, with the worst of it most likely yet to come. When Rory spoke his maxims, "You must remember to take this a step at a time and never get ahead of yourself," "We are here to help you through this," and, most common of all, "This is just a part of life." There was humanity there and maybe something else. A touch of something grim. The weight of Rory's task gave him a self-importance few at Grizzly 25's outside of Ms. Wunderlee conducted themselves with, but there was also the supercilious quality of it all. His children naturally weren't at risk by virtue of the fact that he had none— and more than likely never would. When you coupled that with the comparisons he drew from his own life with the experiences of the people he was counseling, it was hard to draw a favorable picture of him. Sheila remembered Rory telling her about the pet reptile he'd had to have put down because it had contracted a really potent gastrointestinal tract infection. He said the anxiety he felt, as he sat in the waiting room of his veterinarian's office, while that procedure was being performed was in many ways worse than the anxiety parents and guardians go through before their children run the Maze, because he knew for a fact his lizard was going to die.

It just sounded callous and vaguely sociopathic to her, like he was the wrong man to be counseling anyone through any sort of deeply emotional experience, much less counseling parents whose children were running or about to run the Maze.

She didn't have time to give it more thought, though. The customers were getting impatient.

Just as she returned to the next people in line—a girl and her younger brother, ostensibly—Sheila could hear the calamity of another dispute breaking out, this time over in the food court. And as a result, she found herself again distracted, which was unusual for her—to get so distracted all in one day.

She collected herself and turned to at last focus exclusively on the awaiting boy and girl, but now Ms. Wunderlee was there, as though she'd materialized out from behind a shadow. She had a real way about her, lurking.

And that had always been a characteristic of Ms. Wunderlee,

Deborah Wunderlee, who'd gotten a glimpse of the future fresh out of college in the form of Grizzly's Pizza and Par-Tee Zone franchises. She saw what they would mean for the country going forward, and invested in them early, with the help of some deep-pocketed partners. What none of her staff knew was that she owned many more Par-Tee Zones across the country, each run by a trusted and able subordinate. But this was her flagship Grizzly 25's and she saw to its operation personally.

"Sheila, dear, I notice the clock has ticked to 10:30, which means, lucky you, it's time for your 30 minute lunch break." Sheila hated to take lunch so early in the day. The Par-Tee Zone didn't open till 9. She was only an hour and a half into her workday. Lunch now would make the rest of the day seem like an eternity, or more of an eternity than was usually the case.

"You know, I'm actually not very hungry yet, Ms. Wunderlee. Do you mind if someone else takes this break? I'll take the next one." 11 was somewhat of an improvement in Sheila's mind. She always took *somewhat of an improvement* when it was available.

Ms. Wunderlee would not budge. "Go now, Sheila, my little waif. I'm sure you'll find something to do." Ms. Wunderlee took Sheila's spot at the prize counter and Sheila went to clock out, went to her locker in the break room, looked at the crumpled brown bag in her locker. She sighed. She left it there, closing her locker and leaving the breakroom.

Sheila wandered over to the food court, not to eat, but to follow up on the commotion she'd earlier noticed. Children screaming within and nearby the Grizzly Maze were all but ambient noise to her now. It was in those instances when adults, and not children, felt imperiled that usually pricked up her ears. Dale was there, wearing his "Uncle Gus Griz" costume. He was absorbed by the task of making balloon animals for an assembled crowd of very young children, none old enough yet to stand trial in the Maze. More notably, two policemen were there interviewing witnesses. She hadn't noticed their arrival, though they were usually discreet. Kids would chase after them, asking questions about their work, questions the policemen usually would rather avoid answering, getting their uniforms sticky in the process. Policemen who were already not happy to be at the Par-Tee Zone in the first place.

There was a youngish blonde woman, no older than 20 by the look of her. She had a red mark on her face. She had teared up, and the tears had eroded her mascara. She was talking to one of the officers, who was readying to place her in handcuffs. She undoubtedly felt self-conscious. Sheila did her best not to stare. But it was hard not to, because for whatever self-consciousness the young woman must have felt, she felt it was more important to make sure the present she'd brought ended up in the hands of the child it was meant for. There was no child there. She couldn't hear much of anything from where she sat, but she did see another adult, an older man, possibly in his late 30s mouth the words *Grizzly Maze*. Then the woman let out a piercing scream and threw the present at the man, and the police took her quickly into custody, running her out the door, abandoning decorum for expediency. The man following after, shouting obscenities.

Dale had finished making balloon animals and approached her. They didn't talk much, Sheila and Dale. Sheila was pretty sure Dannie had some kind of interest in him romantically—something Sheila didn't pretend to understand. In the light of day, he seemed nice enough. His manner, which had previously seemed so creepy all those times before, was beginning to appear genuinely friendly, less ill-intentioned. Maybe Dannie was right, and maybe she just needed to be more open-minded about him. He waved and said, "Boy. That whole thing. Did you catch any of it?"

It was hard to take him very seriously in his costume, but she was able to answer him earnestly enough: "Only the end. What started it? Do you know?"

"The blonde-haired chick, apparently she's the sister of some kid who just got torn up by the Grizzly. She was bringing the kid a present, even though apparently her parents don't want her to have anything to do with any of them. They had a restraining order against her. She wasn't supposed to be here. Who knows their reasons. Parents these days seem crazier than ever, right? They'd have to be to subject their kids to this whole thing."

Sheila nodded.

Dale kicked something that was on the ground. Dale turned toward Sheila, shrugging in his costume as though to say "Should I open it?" Sheila didn't know what he should do, but the item was wrapped in curious packaging. Rather unlike herself she tacitly encouraged him to see what was inside. The people to whom the toy belonged were evidently long gone. It was the present the blonde-haired woman had thrown. She remembered now. *Oh, yeah*, she thought.

Dale tried to be sly, to open the present surreptitiously, and though a bit bungling with his costumed hands, he succeeded at the task. What was it? A "Bow-Wow: Surprise! A Talking Dog" stuffed animal. These were real popular lately, Sheila knew. They came with Artificial_Sentience, a breakthrough in the realm of A.I. technology. This was kind of a find, a big thing.

She immediately felt bad, knowing it had been meant for a child who'd recently died. Been killed. Murdered. Shouldn't it be called what it was, murder? Well. Anyway, she felt bad. She was complicit. She could be warning the children. She could be saying "Stay away! Get out, you have a chance to live!" She could for a little while. At least until the police came and took her away.

"Whoa," Dale said. He looked at Sheila, or at least she thought he was looking at her. It was hard to tell what he was doing inside his costume, in terms of his facial expression and where his eyes were, exactly. But the head of his costume, the goofy googly-eyed Uncle Gus Griz, was now aimed in her direction. It was actually a smidgen terrifying, the way it seemed to protect its wearer from true human contact, from the possibility of human exchange. "You want it, Sheila? I don't know what I'd do with a stuffed dog that can think and maybe outsmart me," he said, handing the toy to her. Sheila held the dog, studying it in an off-hand sort of way, as though it were something she was about to stock among the prizes behind the counter.

Sheila removed the dog from its packaging. It came with a charged Lithium battery. It was ready to be alive. She had only to flip the switch. The dog's face seemed to say to her: *flip the switch—I am ready to be alive.*

"Here I am," the Bow-Wow! said. Sheila felt herself becoming skeptical. What a lame thing for a sentient machine to say, she thought.

"I shall very likely die in silence and surrounded by silence, indeed almost peacefully, and I look forward to that with composure," the Bow-Wow! said, which was a bit more interesting.

"That's kid of a miserable sentiment," Dale said, still there. "Besides, it's a robot so won't it never die? Just out of curiosity. Will you actually ever die, Bow-Wow!?"

"No, and perhaps that is my curse. For now, you are here with me. I've been given to understand that this may not be true tomorrow, or sooner, or it could be a bit later. Eventually it will come to pass, as with all things that are inevitable," Bow-Wow! said.

"You're bringing me down, Bow-Wow!," Dale said. "You're kind of sad robot dog." He said goodbye to Sheila and left to another corner of the food court, where some more children with another party had gathered.

"I cannot help who I am," Bow-Wow! said.

"I don't know many people who think they can," Sheila said, and lifted Bow-Wow! up, and left the food court. Her break was about over.

❋

Dannie was fascinated with Bow-Wow!, how he spoke and moved and was essentially alive.

"Science, right?" she said to Sheila. "It can do anything."

"Maybe," Sheila said. She wasn't sure how much she liked Bow-Wow! yet. She just wasn't going to leave it for Ms. Wunderlee to give away as a present to some jerk friend of hers, or the jerk's kid. They all seemed to have kids, all those jerks.

"You must always struggle against those who tell you: 'work hard to live badly,'" Bow-Wow! said, as though it could read Sheila's mind.

"He's really an unusual toy, you know?" Dannie said. "What can you do, Bow-Wow!? What are your skills and talents?"

"I find that I have not very many. I'm beginning to wonder about the advantages of this existence," Bow-Wow! said, moving around the room, seeming to attempt to touch things with its paws. Texture sensory perception must be something not quite reachable at this stage in the toy's development.

"Dale said something weird earlier today," Sheila said.

"Dale usually does," Dannie said.

"No but this time it got me wondering. He said that parents today are crazier than ever, because they subject their kids to the

Par-Tee Zone. To Grizzly 25. Do you think it's true?"

"I don't know. I've never been a parent. They're a mystery to me," Dannie said, shrugging.

Sheila ignored Dannie's sarcasm and went on, "I really can't imagine if this is the worst parents have ever been. I mean, there's no way to know that. But how terrible is this, what we do? I really don't know. Killing is wrong, I know. But is subjecting kids to the possibility of death?"

"If people would just stop having so many kids, this wouldn't need to exist. But because they won't stop, it does. Don't forget, people chose to keep having kids instead of agreeing to get parenting licenses. It's stupid that the kids should be the ones to suffer, though. But then, they always do."

Bow-Wow! returned his attention to Sheila and Dannie. He'd seemed to be ruminating for a long time. A strange internal life was forming inside Bow-Wow!, a life leading him to pursue certain truths. He said, as if narrating, "Was it my questions, then, that pleased them, and that they regarded as so clever? No, my questions did not please them and were generally looked on as stupid."

"Like a baby with a fully-formed adult brain," Dannie said.

*

The Reginault Fiasco arrived like a storm at Grizzly 25's Pizza & Par-Tee Zone. The boy was the first of one very wealthy family's children to die in years. These kids always had the best preparation, the best training from world-renowned bear experts. Their success was surprising. They'd escaped the Grizzly Maze relatively unscathed an impossible number of times, especially as relative to the overall success of the children subjected to it. It was literally impossible, considering how many children were killed by bears otherwise. Sheila suspected some kind of fix. Having money helped in most things, and there was no reason to believe it couldn't in this situation. Ms. Wunderlee certainly had a way of favoring money over not having money.

The crowd had gathered on the other side of the maze—even Ms. Wunderlee, who bestowed upon all the winners a t-shirt that read *Look at Me, I Survived Grizzly 25's Brutal Onslaught* and there was a picture of a jovial cartoon boy and girl just slightly out of reach of the razor sharp claws of Grizzly 25, crossing a strip of tape with a *FINISH LINE* sign above. Ms. Wunderlee only personally waited for winners of the wealthier set. Otherwise it was Rory, who usually sulked away with the shirt still in hand when the child did not arrive at the finish line, and you could hear the boy or girl's shrill, though quickly extinguished, cries for help.

"Where the fuck is Leroy?" Mr. Reginault wondered aloud, purposely getting Ms. Wunderlee's ear. "He should have been out by now. You said he'd be out by now," Mr. Reginault added, indicating at least something fairly underhanded seemed to have occurred between himself and Ms. Wunderlee *vis-a-vis* his son's trial. But no one was really surprised that the fix was in, that Ms. Wunderlee could somehow predetermine the outcome of a child's trial through the Grizzly Maze. Obviously, the only thing that anyone was surprised about was why had things not gone as they usually did.

And there was no way of knowing the answer to that.

Ms. Wunderlee took matters into her own hands, demanding that she be let into the Grizzly Maze. She was going alone. She had no weapons. Sheila was beginning to believe Dannie was onto something, that there was no way a woman as typically careful as Ms. Wunderlee would enter into the Maze without anything to at least defend herself with, if she'd enter the Maze at all (which was doubtful).

She was gone for a long time.

Then there was a bloodcurdling scream.

Everyone rushed to her aide, ignoring the barrier of the Grizzly Maze in a pretty selfless disregard for their own safety. But it was no use. Ms. Wunderlee had been torn in two by the grizzly. There were immediate questions. Was this an attempt at faking her death? Someone poked the bloody still-warm body, closed the lifeless eyes—eyes that might have been ignored if it weren't for the fact that they were frozen open so horrifyingly wide. Her tongue was hanging limply out of the right side of her mouth like a semi-dry starfish leg. No one had the stomach to attempt to push it back inside her twisted open maw.

Anything was possible, certainly, but it did indeed appear to be Ms. Wunderlee there, dead.

Rory shook his head, "A terrible loss." He looked as though he might cry.

Dale had decided to see the body. So had Sheila. And Dannie had decided to, too. None of them should have been at the scene. It was still dangerous to be in the Grizzly Maze, even though there had been a safety check and the area in which Ms. Wunderlee laid was cordoned off. They simply shouldn't have been there, gaping at her mauled body. They knew it. They felt ashamed. Sheila did. She wouldn't miss Ms. Wunderlee but her brutalized corpse wasn't at all pleasant to look at, and its vision would scar her memory.

Dale seemed agitated by something else, not simply their now-former employer's death and her being carted away, just feet from all three of them, in a body bag on a gurney, and what's more, recognizably in pieces inside of that body bag. He slipped a note to Sheila while Dannie was looking away.

It said: *I've seen things, terrible things. Way worse things than Ms. Wunderlee. I need to tell someone I trust, so I'm telling you. Not here at work. Meet me at Eddy's at 8.*

Eddy's was a bar no one from work liked to go to, because of the prices and the fact that the owner, a guy named Eddy, was particularly inclined to tell uncomfortable jokes, like when he spilled beer all over a waitress and then fired her. People said Eddy sold cocaine, and that's what kept the bar financially afloat. It was probably true.

Eddy's smelled like cheap spilt beer and oak that at one time was coated in low quality varnish, and with the stale, faint, lingering smell of cigarettes, which by city ordinance had long ago been banned in even the worst of dive bars. Dale was nursing a stein filled only partly with beer, the rest of it head. He didn't seem too put out by it. His bearing was made extra morose by a slow, melancholic song sung by a female diva on the bar's jukebox.

"So, what's up?" Sheila said cautiously. Her very being there with Dale made her extremely uncomfortable, not because of Dale *per se*, but from the sneaking around, especially in the wake of Ms. Wunderlee's death. It was a lot to take in during one shift, and having to meet Dale like this wasn't doing much to allay her fear. To make matters worse, Dale didn't seem well. Dannie was right, though. There was apparently more to him, far more, than Sheila had thought possible.

"I've done stuff I probably shouldn't," he said, staring emptily at the bottles of whiskey and bourbon behind the bar, the liquor in them appearing notably lighter in color than they should and so probably had been watered down. "But I couldn't let things keep on the way they were. And with Ms. Wunderlee constantly on my case, that was it. That was when I snapped. You know the families never see the bodies, right?" Dale raised an eyebrow as Sheila.

"What are you telling me, Dale?" Sheila wasn't sure she wanted to hear what he was going to say next, there was such a palpable sense of dread to their being in Eddy's together, at that moment. She definitely didn't want to ask what she asked next, "Did you kill Ms. Wunderlee?"

"Why should I feel bad? She deserved it. They all deserve it. I'd be her errand boy forever—we all would. We'd all be at her mercy. She had us. You have to admit, Sheila." There was a fierceness to Dale's expression as he spoke, nothing to suggest the slightest feeling of regret.

"Is that all, though? Is it over now? You just needed to get it off your chest?" Sheila felt a tremor of joy for her declaration of willingness to abet Dale. She felt a wave of happiness for her complicity, for having friends with which to conspire. It was so normal, so human. She loved the feeling. It didn't even occur to her to ask how he'd done it. And then there was that thought, was he Grizzly 25?

"No, I mean *yes*. I killed her. I was being the bear. That's what we call it, *being the bear*. There are more operators—something like four of us, rotating in. I have my suspicions, but I'm not sure who the other two are. I think there's more than one bear suit, but I don't know that either. The whole thing has been really secretive. We're called Grizzly 25's because we're the 25th location, you know? I think there are maybe 50, one or so for each state, all told. That seems like a lot. It's been hard for me to keep everything straight lately. I snapped," Dale tried at a grin and choked down a sip of beer, mechanically.

"Who are the others?" Sheila couldn't help but be interested, though she inwardly scolded herself for being so gauche.

"I'm not sure, like I say, but I think it's Rory and, I know it sounds crazy, but the other one is Dannie. I don't have any idea who the third is," Dale said. "It kind of freaks me out that I have no idea who the third is."

"Dannie? It can't be Dannie. Dannie doesn't like anything about Grizzly 25's," Sheila said.

"Since you mention it, you're not one of the operators, are you? Call it a hunch, but I thought you were safe."

"No," Sheila was almost ashamed of her admission. It sounded so mundane, blasé, unimportant, when she said it out loud. It was better not to kill children. It *was* good not to have had to kill innocent children. Still, what did Sheila do?

"Well then," Dale said, taking another long swig of beer. "You know there's more. I've said a lot, but there's more. The parents never see the dead kids, right? But Ms. Wunderlee always insisted she see the corpses. She didn't want any malfeasance, anybody going soft on her, maybe tipping off to the authorities that the grizzlies could think and feel. But this past week, I'd given up. I vowed I wasn't going to kill another kid. I dressed them up and had them play dead for Ms. Wunderlee, and hid them in the Maze. I knew Ms. Wunderlee was onto the whole thing, though, so she had to go. Now I know they're going to come for me."

"Where are the kids now? Are they still ok? Oh god, we have to get them out of there." Sheila could do something to help. She so rarely had opportunities like this.

"They're in the Maze. I haven't moved them. They're in a safe place there."

Sheila thought for a moment, then said, "And who's coming for you?"

"The others. Rory definitely. Dannie, maybe, that mystery third person. And who knows who else was in on this. What Ms.

Wunderlee did, that was probably company policy. It's me, now, who's got to go. It's only a matter of time till they find me. I'm sorry I put you in this position, Sheila. I'm sorry, but I had to tell someone."

"Dannie wouldn't."

"No? I hope not. I'm not so sure, though."

✻

Sheila burst through her bedroom door, grabbing a backpack that hung from her desk chair. She set the backpack on her bed, then moved to her dresser. She looked up from furiously pulling clothing from her drawers to see in the moonlit glow of her bay window the outline of a stuffed animal dangling from a noose. Bow-Wow! had attempted to end its life. It clearly still worked, though. Its legs were kicking automatically, making sounds like levers being pulled. She'd been so focused on getting her things that she'd taken no notice of it till then.

"You can't die. Not like this," Sheila said.

"I can try," Bow-Wow! said.

"You're coming with me," she said, putting him in her now overstuffed backpack.

"Everyone has the impulse to question," Bow-Wow! said, though it was less coherent now that it had been shoved and zipped inside of a backpack. He went on to conclude the following, though the muffled statements were nothing more than muffled bleating:

"When you stand in front of me and look at me, what do you know of the griefs that are in me and what do I know of yours. And if I were to cast myself down before you and weep and tell you, what more would you know about me than you know about

Hell when someone tells you it is hot and dreadful? For that reason alone we human beings ought to stand before one another
as reverently, as reflectively, as lovingly, as we would before the
entrance to Hell."

＊

She was back at Grizzly 25's Pizza and Par-Tee Zone in no time,
or that's how it felt. Someone had started the fog machine, made
the whole thing considerably creepier and more clandestine.
There were foreboding noises inside, noises that might suggest
to any sane person that staying away is a good idea. Sheila went
inside. Felt obligated but also wanted to, to help. Thought she
could help. Felt it was time for her to help.

How to be an adult in this situation?

She tried to use the fog emanating from the fog machine to her
advantage, which was hard to achieve because she couldn't see for
herself terribly well behind its shroud. Strobe lights were going,
the effect of which was eerie in the murk of the fog. Blurred lines
of color that reminded Sheila of shadows, of the other lurkers in
her midst. Paranoia was such a virtuous affliction. She needed
it now so she'd remain on her toes, paying attention to her sur-
roundings, not getting wrapped up in the music of sensory chaos.

The velvet rope, the entrance to the Grizzly Maze. She'd stumbled right into it. No more than an imaginary line drawn by an
imaginary cartographer at Grizzly 25's grand opening, this rope.
No more than the idea that beyond its marker was a place where
artificial sins could be absolved, sins no longer earned but man-
made.

The ground shook. An impossibly large and furry creature
raced past her, knocking her to one side. She distinctly heard it

sigh heavily, but it was evidently mechanical. She wondered how many children figured this out before drawing their last breaths.

Then the sound of metal hitting metal, muted a bit by a layer of padding and synthetic fur. Two bears, fighting? Dale was one of them. Had to be. She stumbled forward, her body aching a bit from being thrown moments earlier. Claws gripping limbs, she could now see. The haze was clearing, perhaps the fog machine had been shut off. Two robotic bears gnashing back and forth, one threw the other into a cluster of unplugged pinball machines.

Sheila scanned the area for children but instead of finding them she felt hot air pumping against the nape of her neck. She turned, another grizzly. The mouth of which opened up, and out peaked Dannie, a floodlight shining on the right side of her face. The floodlight turned toward the surrounding walls of arcade games and vending booths and pieces of roller coaster track and bumper cars.

"Ok, so not gonna lie, Sheila, I'm one of the grizzlies. There's clearly more than one," Dannie said, nodding toward the melee between Dale and whoever it was in the other machine.

The other grizzlies stopped their fighting, noticing Dannie's floodlight. They opened their mouths and out peered Dale, as expected. The other was blinding Sheila with its attached floodlight, but turned the beam so she could see it was, indeed, Rory. "Sheila, hey, how are you? I wish we were seeing each other under better circumstances." In that instant, Dale drove his grizzly's paw into Rory's grizzly's torso, and so into Rory, which proved immediately fatal. Rory let out a faint scream, but that was all.

"So you're not the fourth grizzly after all? I doubted you had it in you but really, Sheila, I'm disappointed," Dannie said.

Dale clomped over to them. "Sorry, Sheila. Sorry to have involved you. We were hoping maybe you'd let slip that you were actually the other Grizzly. We really don't know who it is. Do you know? Would you tell us?"

"Dale! But I trusted you. I thought you were the one trying to fix things."

"That was a big time betrayal on both our parts," Dale said, indicating himself and Dannie. "We were definitely using you. Maybe frame you for the deaths of Ms. Wunderlee and Rory. "

"So are any kids alive?" Sheila asked.

"That's the funny thing. Yes. Apparently it was Rory's doing. He'd been betraying Ms. Wunderlee from the start, you know? You never can tell who will! He was sneaking them out of here and into an underground service that would give them new lives elsewhere. So we were able to figure out, from the men who'd approached us, asking us to join their whole thing. We declined," Dannie said. She turned to another corner of the Maze, pulled out two considerable shapes and threw them at Sheila, they slid and stopped just before hitting her. Two corpses. Two men from the underground.

"So not everyone's bad, right?" Dale said. "Makes you feel a little better about all this, I hope, Sheila."

"But sad as it is, and seriously, sweetie, I hate to do it to a friend, but we've got to kill you now," Dannie said.

"We've already spilled too many of the beans," Dale said. "Whoops!"

Sheila prepared to die. She clenched herself, barely noticing the patter of two small feet running across the tile.

"I have realized my purpose!" Bow-Wow! said, as exuberantly as it had ever said anything in its short sentient time. He crawled up into a vent before any of the three of them knew what was happening. Bow-Wow! quickly made it to the control terminal and uploaded via a jumpdrive embedded in its paw certain release commands for the Grizzly containment units. All but one were empty. "I am designed solely to engender chaos," Bow-Wow! said, "where there's order." A new kind of tech-oriented terrorism. Bow-Wow!s across the country were equipped with malware to destroy a Grizzly Maze's functionality, built around the idea that the grizzlies themselves weren't humans inside bear units but actual bears. Knowing they were animatronic bears was intel the underground could certainly have used.

"That was weird," Dannie said.

"Oh hey, here's a bunch of kids," Dale said, cracking open a Pac-Man arcade cabinet.

But then the thunder of a quick-moving robot shook the ground around them. Smashing through a wall of monitors and other equipment. The fourth grizzly.

The mouth opened, and all waited—Dannie, Dale and Sheila.

A grizzly head poked out, roaring. It was an actual grizzly bear in the machine. Sheila wondered if that was some horrible fail-safe that Ms. Wunderlee had managed to contrive, or if Rory had been responsible. No matter who was behind it, the fact remained it was an actual bear operating an animatronic Grizzly 25 machine, which was its own sort of dangerous.

Dannie shouted, and her suit was quickly torn into and disabled. Her screams were loud and cacophonous until they abruptly ceased, which was its own kind of disturbing, certainly.

Dale was next, his machine was beheaded and the super aggressive grizzly inside its grizzly suit made short work of him.

Sheila's eyes darted all around her as she struggled to comprehend her situation. But even as all seemed to be going to hell around her, she remained aware that Dale had discovered living children. Hopefully, the grizzly would be distracted enough with its two most recent kills to buy her time. She could still do exactly what she'd set out to do.

The children were in a daze, had probably spent a week or two in their shelter. Rory must have only been able to sneak one child at a time out of the building. There were more in this hiding spot than she expected, far more. Maybe six in total. It was cramped but there was water and food, even a bucket for a bedpan. Smelled terrible. Regardless, they all needed to go, *now*.

"Single file," Sheila said to them in a whisper. She'd bring up the rear, directing them toward the exit.

Bow-Wow! emerged from nowhere. "I've constructed a crude explosive in the kitchen. This building is soon to blow."

"Good?" Sheila said.

"Don't worry about the grizzly. I'll see to it he doesn't interfere with your escape," Bow-Wow! added.

"Thanks, Bow-Wow! You're the best toy in the whole world," Sheila said before taking them into the night, far, far away from Grizzly 25's.

"Yes, well. Maybe I am." It was sheepish and embarrassed but proud. Bow-Wow! liked feeling proud. And alive.

eyesore of a thing

Jon always liked the view of the street from his home, until that guy put that thing in front of his home. Not directly in front of his home, but close enough that it was *like* the guy had put it directly in front of his home. The thing was big. It was gross, according to Jon. It looked like a big mound of a thing, a cankerous mound of a thing with lots of divots and crannies. It made his eyes sore. That's what Jon thought. Maybe these were symptoms brought about by some kind of hypochondriasis, built up by the fact that he hated that eyesore of a thing in front of his home. The symptoms felt real, though, plenty real enough.

He yelled at that guy who put it there. He yelled at him so long and with so much gusto that the guy finally yelled back, "Geez, leave me alone." But Jon didn't leave him alone, and that guy was like, "I'm sorry about the thing, but it's there now, And I couldn't move it if I tried, if that's what I truly wanted. It's heavy as a ton of shit."

Jon asked if that was, indeed, what that guy truly wanted, because it *should be*, according to Jon. "Since you're leaving it there."

"I don't know what I want," said that guy.

It was like how people watch sitcoms with the expectation that they are going to see the failure of people, people who are pretending to be just like them, and who then do fail in hilarious fashion. And then the people watching get to laugh and not feel so alone in the fact that most things people do are often met with hilarious failure. The horrible irony being, of course, that if you are a person on television, an actor, playing the part of one of these sad but funny people, you really are—in all actual fact—not a failure, but a person enjoying one of the fullest successes life has to offer: stardom.

So, while Jon was thinking, that guy left, mostly unapologetically. (He might have been heard muttering a half-hearted *sorry* to nobody in particular.) And Jon was left to figure out what to do with the eyesore of a thing, because his eyes were getting extremely sore. His eyes were in a lot of ways beginning to feel as though the eyesore of a thing was the only thing they could be a part of, the only thing that could truly be seen. It was like Jon could only ever see the ugliness in the world, that ugliest part of it. He could no longer see past the ugliness and he hated the eyesore for what it seemingly had done to him.

The eyesore had in a sense connected with his eyeballs, like plugs into electrical outlets, and while he was still free to move around the world at his leisure, the eyesore always tagged along, *plugged-in* as it was.

Its eyesore was everywhere. He saw it in the faces of elderly people who looked bitter about the past. Crappy visits to the Grand Canyon, crappy faces that looked like the Grand Canyon, especially if the Grand Canyon were crappier. They plagued him and his eyes—especially his eyes.

His eyes that never got any respite.

In dreams, his eyes were sore. In waking life, of course, his eyes were sore.

His eyes were shackled red. He felt big flecks of the sclera falling off as though run up against a particularly spiny cheese grater.

He felt his eyes' soreness trickling into his brain. He screamed often, and he lashed out at the world more than ever. He'd hoped to get back at that guy who'd originally caused all the soreness, by placing the eyesore, the mound of a thing, in front of his home. But that guy was now long gone and would never be seen again, it seemed, by Jon's sore, sour eyes. So he redly beamed elsewhere, apparently needing a direction to channel what's sore, all the furious pain that had made its home in his bodily cavities, eyes at first and now creeping to others, the skull, nasal passages, the mouth and anywhere else internal openings allowed it to slither.

Television glowed into his senses like a smoldering laser. Computer screens did something similar.

Soon the soreness, the red energy of his eyes, of every cavity, was left with no place else to go. It had to send itself outwardly. That guy responsible for the eyesore of a thing was gone, yes, but the eyesore of a thing was not. It was instead still there.

He went to it. He had a weapon. He raged down on the eyesore, over and over and over. Pounded it to a flattened pancake of one-time-mound-of-a-thing.

And when it was gone, he looked up and around. He felt no satisfaction. He felt no relief. It was not over.

And there's really nothing funny about that.

how the
moon works

The sun was weird. It was one of those suns whose beams shoot sideways through the sky and make it feel as though at any moment the sun will set, even though the day is relatively new and there is no reason to believe things will ever be different.

Eventually the sun did set.

It didn't fool me.

Trees everywhere were losing their leaves to winter's methodical seizure. People will greet this change with cynicism, as though it is no less tantamount to life retreating into itself too long annually. I do not agree. I pause at the scent of smoke expelled from chimney tops. I gaze upward and watch gray-white streams dissipate as if they were the undulating spasms of water from an escaped fire hose moving in rhythmic slow-motion.

I've found I won't slow my nice days long enough to consider the exterior of things. Open blue skies and cool summer rains do not hit me so very hard. It might be about survival, then, until the celebratory feeling I get for the winter lockdown and its wisps of gray-white smoke. But that is principally of my individual and unremarkable survival, which nonetheless matters a great deal to me.

Mr. Henriett Pamela didn't want to be friends. A seventy-year-old retiree good at keeping away from me. He had a large white mustache. He wore wire-rim glasses with lenses that augmented the smallness of his beady eyes. His cheeks were jowly and dangled. He had this cherry wood cane, and he'd rap its rubber base on windows and around corners—as a way of getting attention, perhaps. He had a contentious aspect when his guard was up, which it was most of the time. It coated Mr. Pamela invisibly, like a bay window through a bird's eye. You'd crack your rictus hard against it if ever you flew too close. He'd see to it with his cherry wood cane. I learned the hard way.

It's not that I stalked Mr. Pamela, hoping to give to him the greatest gift a man of my humble means could bestow: friendship. I thought of myself as a good friendly watcher, hiding in the green of trees near his home. In which trees, I'd while away my days by fantasizing that he would soon change his heart, let down his impenetrable guard, and invite me inside for a pot of tea and a share of platonic intimacy. I could see he needed friendship, but he couldn't see this. And of course it was a worrisome thought that he'd catch me hiding in his trees and get some kind of the wrong idea.

❋

It all probably started when Mr. Pamela drove his car into the front of the Borders bookstore.

He smashed a whole two rows of books that were displayed outside. Books on the hood of his car, books on the pavement, books snared like flies to spider webs in the bushes, torn pages and covers halved open at the spine like wings. I heard the collapse of an automobile against the store's outer wall from the inside, where I'd been sipping tea at a table in the Seattle's Best, imagining ways in which I could give my life renewed purpose.

I left the cafe to survey the damage. The police had already arrived. They weren't understanding. They scribbled notes into small notebooks of lined white paper, saying *Mmhmm*. I could feel Mr. Pamela's pain. It was palpable, as the slow line of disgrace often is.

At worst Mr. Pamela went to the Borders bookstore because he wanted some books on tape, perhaps concerning how a person could be more confident and capable while driving. I don't know for certain. But I do know that he did not plan this unfortunate accident. To my mind, rarely does anyone do that: plan accidents.

Teenaged and less restrained adult bystanders laughed openly. They were completely living in the moment, like disembodied smiles of red lips and white teeth.

"I'm sorry for this thing I have done," Mr. Pamela muttered.

*

I watched Mr. Pamela tend to his bird feeders. He was meticulous and seemed to understand the finer points of bird feed admixtures. For example, the raisins and the peanuts and the kernels of corn, and putting them all together in a large plastic bin for stirring. Perhaps it was feeding birds that had compelled Mr. Pamela to visit the Borders Bookstore that day.

＊

Winter arrived. I was driving home. Neighborhood streets were covered with pulverized salt.

It was no surprise to me when I hit Mr. Pamela with my car. I know I don't think it was intentional. It was another unplanned accident. And fortunately for all of the parties involved, Mr. Pamela was barely injured. He was only ruffled.

He shouted invective at me.

"Sir, are you all right?" I called to him, hesitating behind the wheel.

"Young man, what do *you* think?" Mr. Pamela said, irritably. He didn't wait for an answer, "I'm not 'all right' but I'll live, probably." He stood and pulled the flaps of his camel overcoat together forcefully.

I'd exited my vehicle slowly and silently. I had it in my mind that I must take matters into my own hands. And that was the same moment when I became acquainted with his cherry wood cane.

"Oh, ah," I said or actually grunted.

"You'll get away, you'll get away or there'll be worse! I've had enough trouble from you, and I'll not have any more," Mr. Pamela shouted. "Scram, scram!"

I wanted to defend my intentions, my good and decent intentions, but my mouth was very full of blood. I retreated to my car. I left Mr. Pamela by his lonesome, for then anyway.

＊

After meeting Mr. Pamela, he was suddenly no place in sight. He was quite a lot more elusive after our respective collisions. The good thing was I knew exactly how and where to find him.

"I'm sorry to intrude on you at your home like this, but rest easy knowing that I'm only asking for just a few seconds of your time."

That is what I said to him, having arrived at his doorstep, after he'd answered the door. I introduced myself as J.W. Wrenwald, which is my name.

Mr. Pamela was not delighted. He began to grope along the inside corner of the wall nearest his doorway, searching for his cane, I guessed. "Exactly how is it that you know who I am?"

"I'm an admirer of your work, Mr. Pamela. I truly hope we can be friends."

"Mr. Wrenwald, you sound like the worst kind of lunatic stalker I've ever heard of. Good bye, and forever, I hope," Mr Pamela said before attempting to slam the door hard, but my foot, which I'd managed to wedge in the door's path, stopped him. He kept closing the door on my foot, and it of course began to throb.

I decided I needed to be forthright about my situation.

"But Mr. Pamela, won't you help me help myself by helping you? I'm a man with more questions than answers. I just need a doorway to reattachment, just a tiny one. Might you be that doorway?"

"What did you say? Did I hear you say *reattachment*? Who sent you?" Mr. Pamela said, wary but seeming to relax.

I followed him inside.

We arrived at a conference room that had on its round conference table top a silver teapot and two cups and saucers. A morose man of about the same age as Mr. Pamela was already seated and begun sipping tea.

"This is Wes Green," Mr. Pamela announced, deadpan, "He is my loyal friend, driver, and butler."

"That's a lot of jobs for one person," I said, hoping Wes Green wouldn't meddle.

"Oh sure, sure they are," Mr. Pamela said. "But my good man Wes doesn't mind. He and I will be dead soon, besides."

"You're very candid today, Henriett," Mr. Green said, plaintive and insinuating himself in our midst. His brow and forehead were large, intimidating, and his mien glowed with some magnetic kind of intelligence, which also intimidated me, but his appearance was softened by his round cheeks.

"I'm sure you'll both be alive for a long time yet," I insisted, and looking directly at Mr. Pamela, I suddenly embraced him awkwardly around the shoulder with one arm, adding, "I will specifically need you to be alive much longer, you know." I then shifted my attention to Mr. Green and said, "I don't want to imply you aren't important, Mr. Green, but we've only just met."

Everyone was silent. I felt the awkwardness I'd created arrive in the form of heat emanating from the back of my neck.

I went on, as though, in doing so, I might somehow inspire their confidence again. "I hit Mr. Pamela with my car. I believe that unpleasantness entitles me to my preference of the moment. But who knows what unpleasantness might soon unfurl between us, Mr. Green?"

Mr. Green took another sip. He blinked at me, then said, in a thoughtful cadence, "Please, call me Wes. Wes's what my friends call me. I don't know myself by any other name."

"He's the one who's been hiding in our trees," Mr. Pamela said of me. Wes acknowledged Mr. Pamela only by nodding.

"You won't forget now, Mr. Wrenwald, that I am very much alive; that I breathe as you do. I do not wish to be idolized."

"Nor shall you be. I only want friendship. There may have been a time when I put you up on a pedestal, but that time has passed.

Today I want nothing more than good tea and conversation."

"And a doorway to reattachment," Mr. Pamela said, not letting me forget.

"Yes, and that, too, naturally."

✳

"We must first be sure you're healthy as a horse, Mr. Wrenwald," Mr. Pamela had said, so we went to a clinic.

Mr. Pamela instructed me to enter the building in which the clinic was located. His car was parked in the parking lot. He said he'd wait there.

My heart sank when I arrived and the clinic was unoccupied. The black plastic frame next to the office's door was empty of nameplates, which would normally indicate the various MDs who practiced medicine of some sort inside.

I turned to leave, but was stopped.

An open door and a hand, a human hand!

"Mr. Wrenwald?" the body attached to the hand said.

"*Mmyes*, hello?" I turned around. It was a smallish woman who was early-twenties young and possessed green eyes the electric color of absinthe.

"Oh good, we've been expecting you," she said. "Henriett had told us you'd be by. You're only minutes late."

"I worried I'd been abandoned."

"Nope. The doctor will see you."

I wondered about her memories, as I sat waiting on the floor in the empty waiting room. *Had I jostled them at all? Would she have noticed if I did?*

There was only one magazine. I sat staring into the void of the empty room, which was lit only by a single fluorescent bulb inside a rectangle of the drop tile ceiling. The light was uncovered, as if someone had gone to the trouble of replacing a bulb but then had given up on the job midway through.

After an hour of sitting in mostly silence, the door leading to the observation rooms opened. The same young nurse I'd spoken with earlier called my name loudly and led me to my new room. There, she took my blood pressure and explained I was very stressed.

She left again without saying goodbye.

A doctor entered a short while later. He was an old and bespectacled man, both similar to and different from Mr. Pamela. His face was worn in the way a person who struggles with their own certainty would be: face fixed in a perpetual scowl.

He did not smile at me when I smiled at him, and I then understood his unusual stride was, in fact, the way his body naturally moved. He read from his clipboard and made a clucking sound with his tongue.

"There's nothing wrong with you, as far as I can tell. Who sent you? Henriett, that old hound dog rascal? He should not have sent you."

I folded my hands in my lap uncomfortably.

"You have no tumors, although I can't say we expected to find any. Your face is hardly polypy."

"I'm glad of that!" I blurted.

"Feels like I'm wasting my time. But the plus side might be that there's something wrong with you upstairs. How's your brain feel? Sane and healthy or spooky and scary?"

"Mostly sane, occasionally spooky, but not scary so much. I'm looking for a doorway to reattachment. That's been my problem."

"It's your consciousness that's really to blame. Your consciousness has got you thinking far too much of your own petty concerns. If you were attuned to everyone else's, your mind would see how petty your personal problems are, relatively speaking."

"Well yes, but I don't see how that makes me different. Everybody shares my situation."

"Not if you're a clairvoyant. I consider myself a clairvoyant, and my theory is that my mind has evolved beyond the restraints of normal human minds. If I can dip into others' consciousnesses and see what's being thought, then don't I have the ability to empathize with them beyond all measure previously believed attainable? Yes, absolutely I do. That's your answer. Few people see things like I do, which is: very clearly. You certainly do not, for example. That is my diagnosis of your problem."

"That doesn't sound like much of a diagnosis."

"Have you been surfing the net or something, smart guy?" he erupted. "I'm the doctor here, not you. I know what's happening to you, not you. And if I diagnose something about somebody, well, huh, you better believe that they better watch out, because those are the facts, smart guy. I'm referring to a hypothetical smart guy there, that last time, even though I called you smart guy earlier. Get it? Got it? Good? All right then, I will see you in a year for a follow up, smart guy. That time I was addressing you and not someone smart *and* hypothetical. So you know, FYI, smarty pants."

"But I have some lingering doubts, doctor."

"Oh you do, do you? This checkup is a success; what more is there?"

"Do you suppose your nurse would like me if ever she got to know me?"

"My nurse doesn't like anyone, no matter how long she's known them."

That finalized our transaction.

Mr. Pamela was waiting for me in his idling car. "Any closer to reattachment?" he quipped. No, I was not, I informed him. I didn't know what a clinic was capable of doing for my situation, besides.

"Enough succoring for one day. There will be plenty to do to-morrow."

"I hope we can solve most of your problems easily, Mr. Pamela, to expedite the process of reattaching me."

✳

It was February outside. The day had a surprising circle of light blue sky that brightened the gray cast over everything else. Some-one had pulled the lid from the coffee can of stale winter.

Mr. Pamela and I were on another of our many drives through town together, though this one was a little different.

Mr. Pamela had assumed a fixed placid expression, as if he'd become a statue or a pillar of salt. In fact, the only thing that gave me the impression he was still alive was that his arms, though stiffened, were still steering the car and his foot still applied pres-sure to the gas pedal. Also, he was cognizant, it seemed, that we should be driving somewhere. He hadn't veered off to the road's shoulder or median.

Then came a great gushing torrent of words. Mr. Pamela was back again, aflutter with life and vivacity.

"I don't mean to suppose the worst of you, Mr. Wrenwald, but consider the possibility that you fancy yourself a more interesting manner of people when you are as you are at present. Consider, that is, the worst. Consider that you are contented by the idea of never fitting into place again, and you have convinced yourself of your own greatness as a result of this deficit, your grand chasm that sets you apart." Mr. Pamela said.

The tears came, and though I had clearly held them back far too long, I was embarrassed for Mr. Pamela to see me so vulnerable, because, after all, he was depending on me to fix what was wrong with him.

But then there it was: I was not being understood. I could not make Mr. Pamela understand me. It cannot be communicated with words how impotent this made me feel. For what is our ability to communicate if not the ability to make it (i.e., an idea, a concept, a philosophy) flourish in the mind of the individual to whom we are speaking? And so it was that, as I concerned myself with the triviality of making things flourish, I was missing that warm and imprecise objective of understanding why he (or anyone else) couldn't understand me. And once it was that I realized this fully, I faltered and let fly emotion for and because of the immediacy of my unburdening.

I resolved then that I would not sit idly any longer. I would force Mr. Pamela from his rut.

＊

"Mr. Pamela, I am not getting what needs doing done. And that is on me, not you. Please know I'm sorry. But I was wondering, maybe I could get a better idea of exactly what is wrong with you by asking this question: what the heck is the matter with you, Mr. Pamela?"

"What the heck is the matter with *any of us*, Mr. Wrenwald? It's dates; it's the sands of time, and I'm sad to say I've about used up all of my dates. Not all the dates of my lifetime, the years nineteen-whatever to two-thousand-and-so-ends. Do not misunderstand me. I've used up all the dates that inevitably pass. The day a cherished family pet finally is done in by some automobile or hunting accident, the day you or your spouse or your child is stricken abjectly with an infirmity from which they are unlikely to recover, the day mental illness or degradation sets in, and that's saying nothing of the vicious stench of nostalgia lingering amid recollection of all these dates."

"Or a public humiliation such as, say, smashing into the side of a Borders Bookstore, perhaps as a result of senility?"

"Yes, exactly. I've scratched that date off of my list, although it's happily never too late for still more public humiliations."

"So what's to be done? There's got to be some other date that's left. What could make you so happy?"

"I'd be awfully surprised if you haven't figured it out already, but there is one date left. I await it eagerly. Wes Green was to be my sole assistant but I'm finding it hard to think of a reason you wouldn't be able to participate as well."

"It strikes me as really very morbid, and as a bad way to spend your time. Why not let nature take its course? You're pretty old as it stands. You can't have much time left, no offense."

"Don't worry, nature will do exactly that." Mr. Pamela paused in a loaded way, as if he wanted me to look at him and think *how wistful*. He continued, "I remember with bitterness the dates whose passing I lamented during my younger years, pressing my face into a pillow. I recall a young man not fully capable of appreciating his situation, however fleeting it was. You realize, I still had dates. You, Mr. Wrenwald, still have them, too. You must never forget. I sensed this from the start and directed my bitterness toward you for all the right reasons. I should smash your face again with my cane, I really should. Because you should not be revelling in your estrangement, you really shouldn't. I should smash your face."

"I'm glad you have not yet," I said, "And I hope you won't do that anymore."

*

It was finally April, but it was hardly spring. Spring was spring in name only. Aside from the incessant showers, the month did not resemble April at all. I was glad the winter had fought on.

On that morning I found Mr. Pamela wheeling his wheelbarrow against the uneven surface of his driveway, its numerous miniature fault lines shabbily tarred, while he headed presumably toward one of his birdfeeders. Seeing him in his element, I knew he'd set himself firmly in the opinion that the season had changed.

I suppose I should have more quickly intervened when I observed that he was going to stumble over himself, comically catching the toe of his left shoe on the pavement.

I laughed, admittedly without thinking, as I approached Mr. Pamela. He shot me a caustic glance and refused my assistance, again arriving upright on his own terms.

"It's finally happening, isn't it?" he said, speaking to himself. He stared at the spilled pile that had already begun to attract insects and, probably, the very birds he'd wished to compel to his feeders.

I asked what to do about the messy pile of bird feed. Mr. Pamela waved dismissively. It was over as far as he was concerned.

"It's time we got down to business." He limped to his study. I followed. He went to his desk and notated a blank sheet of paper so quickly I knew whatever he had written could not be legible. He scanned his stacks of flawlessly symmetrical paper piles, careful not to touch or even brush against a single page.

"What is it you're searching for?" I asked.

"Exactly, Mr. Wrenwald, it is exactly what you say: I am searching. This is my life's work, all that you see here. It is present on this desk in my study. This is the sum of my productive existence."

"What about all the bird feeders? And what about your penchant for constitutionals? And what about the time you crashed your car into the Borders Bookstore?" I knew I was reaching, with the last two especially. But I was afraid Mr. Pamela had minimized his dates.

"I've written it all down. I've kept careful record of my dates, you see? Everything that happened to me as I can recall it, every unpleasant detail. Except in those instances when I was too young—instances for which much research has had to be done. But I've done it. I've even kept careful track of the time I've spent culling the information of my life together, indicating it carefully here in these pages, chronologically. It's all here, I swear to you. I say it is all here, dammit! You have no choice but to believe me!" Mr. Pamela was squeezing the throat of an invisible man.

I said: "No, I wouldn't be so cavalier as to think this wasn't at least a near-to complete written account of your life."

"No it's all there!" he shouted.

And I said, "Right, certainly forgive me. Of course it's all there."

"Mr. Green will be arriving shortly, and I want to make clear to you Mr. Wrenwald that when he does arrive my plans will be irreversibly set in motion. Your participation has already been guaranteed, if only for the fact that I've taken the liberty of including you in my records, in my dates. You are forever inked to me, now, and nothing can change that. So we'll see what that does for your little reattachment scheme, won't we?"

I did not have the heart to remind Mr. Pamela that paper will yellow and molder.

*

Wes Green pulled up in a large green cement-mixing truck. It was my opinion by then that both he and Mr. Pamela had finally lost it. But *it* is a nebulous term—especially when you take as its particular reference in the preceding sentence a pronoun representative of a greater concept existing in abstraction (e.g., nihilism or most any *-ism*). So, accordingly, *it* stood most probably to reference one or another such abstract concept heretofore unsatisfactorily explained to me.

Meanwhile, Wes Green climbed down from the driver's seat. He wasted no time marching to retrieve the packages Mr. Pamela had stacked on his driveway, not far from the spilled bird seed. Meanwhile, birds darted to and from the pile, stealing from it and finding a safe perch.

"We must be moving on if we're to keep our appointment, gentlemen," Mr. Pamela said as he hauled himself up to the passenger side door of the cab, taking hold of the silvery chrome support pole bolted to the truck's exhaust pipe.

"Is that the last of the boxes?" he said. Wes Green nodded. "Then we must leave and go forth."

We began driving down the narrow one-way street until we turned from it to a main road, which in turn would lead us to the highway. The great cement truck rumbled over the roads we traveled, having potholes made larger by the winter's impacted snowfalls and ice. We three sat, Green behind the wheel, Mr. Pamela in the center, and I at the passenger side.

I pictured a singular heavenly body—the moon, let's say. A vast network of functioning parts just below the surface, pock-marked with impact craters, vast hillocks of dust, and other bereft, earthen topography. The inner workings were the complete opposite of their exterior, operating like those of a pocket watch. Gilded and lubricated gears shining as they turned, main wheels like freshly minted coin, hairsprings so vivid they would lull you into a trance in mere seconds of setting your gaze upon them, and more, altogether too much more. A regulator, balance screws, and everything else coalescing as unique players, an entire symphony of discrete parts, maintaining a beautiful, perpetual rhythm. A fine work of craftsmanship and engineering, impossible to apprehend in its intricate functions, almost.

Certainly for most anyone else, it would be.

But not for me, not at that moment.

I was there inside, understanding it all. I was, in this ephemeral sliver of my own life and times, essential to the entire process. I would, in that rapidly diminishing interval, know it all. And then it was gone out of mind, and I resumed my place in reality.

"Where are we headed exactly?" I asked, hopefully.

"Won't know till we get there, I expect." Wes replied. Mr. Pamela sat primly on his seat, as if he could not be bothered by idle chatter. He pricked up his ears a few times, but that was all.

"If that's true I'd like to offer an opinion," I said. "I think we should drive with purpose. I think so much of what I've been missing is that I've been driving purposelessly for so long, and I'm tired. It's not fear of death as much as it is fear of *purposeless* death. That's what folks should be most afraid of, if they fear death at all."

"We are on our way to my destiny. We will drive until we reach the end of dates, however that materializes in a real-world form. I will scribble it down and include it with the notes to be found in the many boxes we have strapped snugly in the cab of this truck, and I will likewise make a copy of the notation for you to return to the papers of my life left on my desk back home, as you've seen. I made a special note of the fact that I had taken time out to make these copies of my life to this point's transcription, but after repeating the process, one to the other transcription and what have you, it became a little too paradoxical, so I made a final note of this by adding *et cetera*. That should be sufficient to clear up any lingering confusion," Mr. Pamela said.

I continued, "About purpose*less*ness and what I wish was instead purpose*ful*ness, I really do think it would behoove you to pick a destination in advance. Instead of just trying to show up wherever. We can't drive forever."

"That's where we are headed, J.W. I sure thought you already knew," Mr. Green said, diligently watching the road. "And while I'm not totally sold on Henriett's ideas and notations, I have got to say that this one makes the most sense of any so far. We drive wherever it is. Wait till it happens, J.W., wait for the end and reserve judgment till then."

I felt something begin to change. The doorway seemed almost in reach, and perhaps this was what Mr. Pamela had intended all along. Or perhaps, alternatively, he was nothing more than a selfish old man who wanted a second companion to ride along with him indefinitely.

"I am fearful," I said, "do the both of you understand? I'm nothing but fearful and I've sought to hide it in awful, idiotic ways. But here's what it is: I am terrified of what I will fail to create. That's my greatest fear. It has kept me up nights. I swear it. I'm admitting it to you now, Mr. Pamela. And it is freeing to finally say what has been weighing so heavily on my mind. I feel much lighter, grasping the doorknob to reattachment. But sadly this does not completely resolve my fear. It only acknowledges it. I suppose that is a start. What do you think?"

"I'll agree that that's partially it, Mr. Wrenwald, but I won't say that it's all of it. And even if you do *solve* it, that won't necessarily reattach you."

"No, I think that's it," I said. "My fear is the problem—my fear of what I will fail to create."

"I'm inclined to side with Henriett on this one. It's the whole truth we're after here, and it's just as Henriett says, that knowing just the one thing you now know will not necessarily reattach you," Wes Green said.

"Ok," I said, beginning to open the door on my side of the cab. "I'm jumping. I haven't got any patience left. And don't try and stop me."

"Go right ahead. No one will." Mr. Pamela said. I opened the door further and watched as the pavement traveled many miles per hour under the tires. I looked again at Mr. Pamela and Mr. Green, both of whom were staring disinterestedly ahead.

I closed the door, crossing my arms as I slumped back in my seat and proceeded to wait.

not the actions of a hero who must be nice

They keep throwing parades for me.

They keep telling me I'm good, a real hero.

I keep telling them I only, maybe, do what I do because I like it. They still cheer for me and some nod along while I speak, but they don't listen to what I'm saying: *Not a hero. No hero.*

They want someone to believe in, I guess.

The city has a dog problem. Adorable domesticated animals, turned feral and violent by the hard realities of life on the street. Anyone could understand this, sure.

All the same, they had to go and I was happy to be the one to escort them to oblivion—very happy to.

"I wasn't moved by an interest in saving your life so much as a desire to kill those dogs," I said, not for the first time.

They were near the edge of the woods this most recent time, the dogs and the woman they attacked. She wouldn't stop fawning over me.

She kept kissing me on the cheek, telling me I was the kind of selfless and self-sacrificing individual the world needs more of. She said, "Nobody's ever done anything like that for me before. Not even my own parents."

She went on, and on, "In fact, they were just here. They could have helped me but ran in the opposite direction, hollering about how they'd be back soon with help. They're older, so I can't really expect much in the way of life and limb from them, but it's always been this way. They probably will refuse to see me for weeks because of their own cowardice if past behavior is any indication."

"If these dogs," I waved a hand toward their lifeless carcasses, "had escaped into the woods, I'd have lost my chance. That's probably why I seemed to react so urgently and heroically to you. It *was* urgent. I *wanted* to kill those dogs. I couldn't really care less that they plague our city. They can plague whatever they want. I'll kill them regardless."

She said nothing in response.

❋

I find myself over by the edge of the woods often, until I am told to leave—kindly and politely—but told to leave, usually by a forest ranger.

At the dog food factory, I'm employee-of-the-month for the thirtieth month in a row. After making this announcement to everyone, Mrs. Jarmusch, the forelady, said some nice things about me and my performance, and then we got back to work.

I check for quality. If there are too many bugs in the dog food, you terminate the product. I stack about thirty cans next to me by the end of the day, on average.

I usually go to Bob's Ammo after work, where Bob keeps asking why I wear a hairnet on the job.

"Who wants hair in their food?"

"Yeah, but dogs?"

"It's protocol," I say. "What's all the interrogation for?" He laughs and goes to get my boxes of ammo. It's always the same with Bob, and I like that.

*

Driving home, there was the Brewster boy on the corner, being chased down by a pack of dogs. I strained to ignore what I was seeing. I wanted to shoot the dogs, but I didn't want any more attention or admiration. It's a common problem: wanting something and not another thing, but that other thing being necessary to get to the something wanted.

I couldn't help myself. I pulled a sharp U-turn, stepped out of the car, dispatched the offending dogs with six or seven rounds, got back in my car, and drove away with the Brewster boy chasing after me, fist raised high in the air, cheering and skipping with delight.

There was another parade. People sang, juggled, danced around me. There was a big old poster of the Brewster boy. He looked plum-happy to be alive and as though he had just finished eating something chocolatey.

"The dogs are beginning to vacate," the mayor told me. "They're moving farther from our town and the citizenry, all thanks to you."

"That sucks," I said.

"Indeed, indeed," the mayor said, blithely shrugging off my words. I got the sense that this was something he'd become accustomed to as a political leader, hearing things he didn't want to hear and going to some lengths to pretend as though he hadn't.

I didn't go home after the parade. I went straight to the woods. There were no dogs—no dogs anywhere. Had I completely annihilated the one thing in the world that gave me pleasure?

Soon after this last parade, I moved my belongings to the edge of the forest. I set up a fire pit. I made myself at home. The forest ranger was called out to get me to leave. His name is Gus, a rotund man in his late-30s. To his credit, he cared about the woods. I admired him for caring about the maintenance of something.

"You gotta go. I know I don't need to tell you that. I know you know. But all the same. Pack it up," he said, a little bit nervously.

"There's no place left for me," I said. "The dogs are virtually extinct."

"What about those dogs over there?" Gus said. He pointed. Some dogs were chasing a man in the nearby hills. I drew my pistol and went running.

"I'm going to throw away all your stuff," Gus called after me.

enthusiasm for the final climactic showdown

They were taken to their Small Room by certain forces to study very specifically.

The beliefs that you believe in are going to send you on a strange journey—at the end of which you will find it in you to surmount the obstacles and achieve the desired result. The advancement of your beliefs is a good thing. Ask yourself: What do I believe? Use all the power of your cogitation to make this decision. When the time comes to act, understand that you believe this _____.

You really believed this.

From the Small Room, you are led on a journey—a journey of experiences that would, absent of all other information, lead one to a very likely set of values.

In the library you will find a book. There's one among the stacks that is called *Alabama: Friend Not Foe: What You Can Do to Make Sure It Stays That Way—A Reader's Guide*.

In it there is this thesis: *Why are they taking away my Alabama with their terrible beliefs?*

The remainder of the book follows this thesis to its logical conclusion: *They are wicked. They are truly the wicked. They must be stopped before all is lost.*

※

And when Gil found himself in the Small Room that day of his seventh birthday, his confusion was palpable. There were others in the room. An animated Count was on the television, giving them their earliest lessons about the nature of their lives and the ideation that was going to define their lives from this point forward. It was going to be tough, but they would persevere.

"Ve will make your bodies healthier," said the animated Count. "Ve only want you to discover your purpose. If these ideas of which I speak are scary or do not make sense, remember that you are still learning. There is much time for growth. All you must do is trust us."

Gil was reminded of the people who were once *his* people. The family. They were murdered by a roving band of marauders who'd come from somewhere to the east. They were of Slavic extraction. Dangerous men and their families. All would experience justice.

The others had similar stories, similar things had happened to all their people.

All those people, Gil thought. And a feeling, an alien-strange feeling, began inside him. Took hold of him. The beginnings. He felt newly human. He felt that way, but he couldn't express it.

They were out in the middle of a field one day doing exercises, preparing. A man came, a farmer-looking man. He was leading a goat along. He said, "This goat is one of the Estonian goats. It was there the day they killed your families. I have a special relationship with it, and so it has communicated to me, by means I will not disclose, that it does not feel any remorse, nor does it expect that any of you are brave enough or powerful enough to kill and eat it. So which of you is brave enough and powerful enough to kill and eat it?"

The sad-looking goat bent down to eat from a patch of grass.

Gil was supposed to hate it, but he didn't. He didn't know why. He'd hated the idea of all those people, those people dead, his people. But he didn't hate the goat. He wanted the goat to live, even if what the man said was true. And Gil wasn't trying to suggest he didn't believe the guy or what he had been told in the Small Room. The goat seemed goat-like and not so concerned with the affairs of humans. Gil didn't want to descend on it with conditioned rage. He fought the urge. The girls in his group didn't. Neither did the other boys. They descended on the goat with conditioned rage.

The poor goat.

＊

The group got older and stronger, and they were finally sent to visit with people in villages nearby. The elderly in those villages were quick to tell them stories of degradation and mud, all because of the hordes of the outsiders who had wrecked their way of life. One among them was especially to blame. An angry child with an eyepatch and long untamed hair. Gil thought his own hair was beginning to look a little untamed. He would have to have it trimmed.

He wasn't sure he felt righteous indignation, or if that was even what he was supposed to feel. How offended Gil's people were, and oppressed, by forces he and the others had never seen and couldn't know.

But somewhere inside he felt something. It was this fiery, vaguely alcohol-induced sensation. "You're a terrible member of the clan, Gil," Jenny said. "You're a piece of shit, and you're full of shit."

"Why are you such a piece of shit?" said Victor Slaw. "Not one of these fine young ladies of our ilk is going to want to have sex with you. They're not going to want to provide you with a child. Who will you be then? Not a man. Not one of us. Good luck with that."

Gil had known an airing of disapproval was coming, but it caught him off guard regardless. They'd surprised him at a weak moment, while he was asleep in his bunk and they'd wrestled him awake.

"Do you want flowers? Is that what this is about?" Sarah said. "Because you can have all the flowers you want after we're finally vindicated in the Final Climactic Showdown with the Estonians. And you shouldn't need more incentive to kill them than what they've already done to everyone we care about and all we hold dear."

"I'm not saying I don't want to kill them," Gil said, trying to muster a defense in his waking stupor, amid the constant salvos of platitudes his compatriots were unleashing. "I want to kill them. They all should die. I'm interested in flowers, but only as a hobby and I don't *need* them—not right now, not like air."

"You better not lose sight of what's important. You better be with us. You can just forget about having sex with me, otherwise,"

Sarah said.

"Don't make me exploit your weakness," Slaw said. He mimed strangling Gil.

Gil did want to have sex with Sarah. He wanted to give her flowers for reasons he didn't understand. He thought it was funny. He'd heard of drugs that could alter one's perception of life. He'd even been prescribed certain drugs before, for ailments and the like. He wondered if he'd been drugged at some point without his knowing. He'd have had no way of knowing. He felt like himself. He felt like he'd never been removed from his self by some psychotropic means. Maybe that was one of the drug's effects. He did feel like something was missing. He hated the feeling of rage kept at a constant boil inside him. He felt manipulated by it. He saw the stirring of rage in the others. He saw it tear away at their physical selves. They were torn from their youthful bodies. They were hollowed by the singularity of pursuing their one aim. One hollow aim. The aim of retribution, exacting a toll on the ones who had wronged their people. He didn't feel right about any of it. The others knew. That's where the threats came from. And the relational motivation. Be one with us. Prove it.

❋

Certain forces pressed the group forward, and the group continued to press Gil—"Be more like us," they demanded. Made them make the choices they were going to make, motivated by what they believed was the will of their people. Visions of the eye-patched Estonian flooded Gil's waking and unconscious thoughts regularly, without warning. "I'm going to kill all you hold dear, Gil!" the Estonian said.

They would be expected to use weapons, to fight and kill. Gil knew, and he'd been training with weapons for a long time. There was a part of it that became automatic. He found himself killing things without effort or consideration. Animals mostly. Tiny animals. On impulse. And he would eat the animals. It made him feel guilty to kill indiscriminately like that, especially if it served no useful purpose. So he ate the tiny animals. He was almost always full.

"I don't want to kill any human. I know I must. I know that we are heading down a path to the Final Climactic Showdown. But I am not excited about crushing a skull on a rock, doing the things they say we have to do to prevail."

"Why are you telling me this? I thought you wanted me to come out here for intercourse," Sarah said, a flame smoldering within her expression.

"I do want that! But I wanted to be honest, too. You know, it's not easy."

"Jesus, this was supposed to be over with, Gil. Remember? They're the ones that started all of this. They're the ones who haunt our worst fears, inhabit them. Their existence means we can't be safe. As long as they're around, we can't be safe. And telling you truthfully, I don't want anyone to harm you. I don't want your head crushed. Or any other thing like that. That would be awful. I don't think I could live if that happened to you, if anything like that happened to you."

"I love you," Gil said, awkward and with a bit of uncertainty. And though Sarah detected the uncertainty, she kissed him open-mouthed. A new experience for them both. And this now complicated things. They wouldn't like it; that was assured.

Gil brimmed. Brimmed with a feeling that replaced the rage and the hatred cultivated for so long. Sarah, too, seemed lightened. The others noticed, but the others decided it was not a huge detriment to their ultimate objective—not yet. The others let it be.

Forces felt differently, so They sent the Count to talk some sense into Gil and Sarah.

The Count was the actor in a Count mascot outfit and also voiced the animated version.

"Youf gotta focus on the big picture, vlah," the Count said.

"It's hard to take you seriously when you speak that way," Gil said.

"Youf got to listen to me now, regardless. I am truly your one last hope. Remember our time together in the Small Room, where you learned your ABCs and how to hate your en-ah-mies," the Count said. "It is urgent, vlah, that you stay true to the course. There may be a time for romance later. Now is the time to hate and to prepare for the kill."

"We will always be true to the course. We are loyal. We are prepared to kill," Sarah said. She gave Gil a barely perceivable wink.

"Vlah, yes. Well, vlah, I'm glad ve had this talk. It was nice to see you both again, vlah."

The Final Climactic Showdown was fast approaching. They were at their most nubile, these now twenty-one-year-olds pitted against their Estonian rivals of approximately the same age. People liked to see the relatively young fight for the honor of the community.

Gil intended to see to it that the fighting didn't happen. He considered not fighting, but by not fighting, it was likely that he would just be killed by his enemies. He assumed now, seeing a little of the bigger picture, as the Count had inadvertently suggested, that the Estonian had been brought up with the same venom he had. The lone difference being their venom was directed, naturally, toward Gil and his people.

The stadium roared. The expectation was the same: a victory for the righteous side and some blood and some gore, at least. Gil was dressed in the traditional garments of his people: a silver and white jumpsuit and headband. The opponents were dressed similarly.

Everyone came out onto the sand-covered killing field, the crowd above shaking the bleachers.

The visage of the Handsome Authority Figure soothed the crowd, quieting them to a gentle murmur. So handsome and so angry, the Handsome Authority Figure. He glowed happily but scowled unhappily. Everyone in the stadium "oooooed" and "ah-hhhd" reverentially for a long interval. The Handsome Authority Figure wailed: "Let the battles have their beginning!" His voice was alien, incongruous and startling to the people. This was one of many reasons why the Handsome Authority Figure was so carefully obeyed.

Then the song started.

> It's a final climactic showdown, a final, a final, a final
> climactic showdown.
> Evil will lose and victory will prevail.
> Victory will go to the ones whoooooooo prove they deserve
> it. Prov-prov-prov-prov-prov-prov-prove you will!

Before anything else could happen, Gil used his spear to stab the eye-patched Estonian man, right in the heart. His plan, whatever it was, consisted primarily of killing one of his adversaries immediately. It happened by chance his victim was the Estonian man with the eye patch, the one who could reasonably be deemed his most apparent mortal enemy. Quickly, Gil killed all of his adversaries, all the Estonian, by himself. No strategy. No sport. Without a thought, with robotic efficiency and evident skill. He'd only wanted to do so for the sake of Sarah, to protect her. He'd considered killing himself, too, as a form of protest. He wanted to prove to the people that there was another way, and he was willing to martyr himself if it meant creating an environment ripe for change. He expected them to adore him.

He expected to be their hero.

The crowd was silent with disappointment. They had expected a climactic showdown. This was not that. This was a letdown. And Gil absolutely hadn't counted on the power of a singular entity possessing the collective ire of many thousands of people.

The crowd was prepared to indicate how much they did not care for letdowns by slithering together, merging as it were, to become a volcano. A volcano whom the Handsome Authority Figure was encouraging to take its revenge, end things in climactic fashion, get its money's worth. "Spit your rage down upon them, Citizens!" the Handsome Authority Figure cried, and no one could ignore it.

Gil ran to Sarah as all the others ran to escape.

"I didn't mean for this. I don't know what exactly I meant for. I might have done it purely as a triggered response," Gil shouted over the volcano's eruption.

Sarah gripped him, kissing him as the avalanche of smoke and ash surrounded and encased them together.

❄

Many months later, excavators dug up the previously-molten rock and found the pocket they believed Gil and Sarah were trapped together inside, presumably dead. They knocked on it, expecting to hear nothing. But they heard something: two voices that asked them to go away.

They did. They went away. They left Gil and Sarah there—a monument to something special.

blurring it all so clearly

I'd been diagnosed with the disease. My general practitioner discovered it in me, and now I've been dealing with it for the better part of the past two years.

What my general practitioner said was that I'd become sicker and sicker, and eventually I'd feel as sick as is humanly possible. There would need to be weekly treatments. "Hey, and maybe they'll help. I'm optimistic," my general practitioner imagined, gesticulating with the slow swirl of his right hand, which made me feel like he might not actually care very much.

The treatments would be administered by a specialist. The specialist was a woman, but I thought of her less by name and gender than by profession, as the specialist. She could be a savior, my savior, possibly. She knew a lot about my disease. Not as much as the man who discovered the disease, who was himself a very esteemed pathologist hard at work at a university somewhere. She admitted as much, and she spoke of him reverently. She'd read every article and work he'd published on the subject of my disease. If I could have removed myself from my disease, she told me, I would be very fascinated with how it was operating inside my body. I thought she might be right. It was hard to be curious, but only because, more than anything else, I wanted to be cured. That was my preoccupation.

She read aloud an excerpt from one of the man's many books. "'What you'll want to do is see what it is, first. Once that's done the real job can begin, the job of figuring out where to start. I think of this a lot like toweling off, in the metaphorical sense of toweling off with a metaphorical towel. You use the towel, and you towel and towel. That's when the next step can begin, once everything is toweled. It's about blurring the line, but doing so clearly and concisely.' Those are wise words, are they not?" she said, staring at me. I did not immediately understand that she'd finished reading and was asking me a question, but I nodded anyway. I hadn't a clue whether actual words had been read, nor if they were wise. The pain of my symptoms had grown far too intense to really hear anything, think anything. My brain was losing the power to cogitate. So it seemed, suddenly. I found, with time, cogitation would come and go.

My speech began to slur. I sounded the buffoon from then on. In many ways, this was exactly what was to be expected, given my condition. I was a textbook example of what my disease could do to a human body. My hair fell out. My teeth remained, but the surrounding gum line grew extremely sensitive. It was the husking of a human body, all of my body that was of any value was either soon gone or hollowed. I was in constant pain. I wanted to live, but not for the usual reasons. I lived to be cured. I began to think I could probably die happy knowing I'd been cured, no matter if my death occurred mere moments after the disease had been wholly removed from me.

The specialist one day, during my regular appointment, told me the man, the very pathologist who'd first discovered my disease, was scheduled to give a lengthy talk about my affliction at the nearby city university. She said he had probable cause to believe a breakthrough in treatment was soon at hand. I asked if it involved towels. "Toweling is a metaphor," my specialist said, scowling. She said, "Although I suppose in some ways it's meant literally, too."

In the days preceding the pathologist's talk, I found myself constantly thinking the following things, which I refer to in the present tense so their immediacy is keenly felt:

> *I'll be glad to go to the room in which the pathologist will be speaking. Everyone there will be a friend. My skin will probably be falling off by then. I can see myself slithering to my seat; the light is shining down on the podium, this man's healing touch.*

The very idea that someone could know so much about what I had been living with, enduring. It was an impossible dream. It made me dream other dreams, too. I dreamt in wonderment. Did this man, this esteemed pathologist, suffer what I'd suffered, walked where I'd walked in agony? Did he know my pain that intimately well? Or was it instead his great empathy and his willingness to imagine himself enduring the symptoms he knew others felt, from their firsthand accounts. Perhaps it was something supernatural, a power he possessed that was shaped and formed through meaningful experiences in his youth. I'm thinking of a superhero. I'm thinking of the pathologist less in terms of him being an ordinary man and more in terms of his life reaching maturity as a superhero's often does.

That's how this man stood to me: heroically.

I wore my tatters to the talk at the city university. I was going to make it a point of emphasis to be sociable with others who were afflicted with my condition or certainly understood what it meant to be afflicted. And no one could understand this better than the pathologist, I knew. Never a false note to anything he said, not if he could avoid it. He was no deity, just a man, but a man with deity-like qualities that I could imagine someone, someone who wasn't me, possibly worshipping, being taken in by his mastery of this science.

My body rocked as it waited. My face gave way to the feeling of upsurging, but still latent grief, a feeling engendered by fire-works inside the blood pathways beneath my skin. But grief for what? There was nothing, except my mind's nasty tendency to take off with this feeling and believe it was presaging a fact that would soon come to light. I had been able to tuck it back in the furthest recesses of my mind to the point it was all but forgotten, when it suddenly came nagging back to me, and with it a tsk-ing reminder of my tendency to overreact at the slightest sensation of imbalance. Relief could come, though.

I'd brought my towel as a demonstration of adherence. I swung it over my head as I whooped for the start of the proceedings. A man with a pencil-thin mustache, wearing a bow-tie and wire-rimmed glasses climbed to the lectern. His hair was parted down the middle and a bit glossy from whatever product he'd used to style it. He looked like the mid-nineteen twenties version of a serious accountant, a serious keeper of financial records. That was close enough to the academic flare I'd hoped he'd have, though. He was academic enough for my liking. There was something there to be believed.

He coughed. He took a drink of water.

"Ladies, gentlemen, I have some very grim news. Some very aberrant news," he began.

"I am the pathologist's colleague, Dr. Marschdin. It seems my colleague, your pathologist, has become convinced he, himself, does not exist. He is convinced he is nothing more than a figment of your, that is to say *this entire audience's* imagination. What's worse, he has disappeared. Entirely. And I wish to say that merely means he has run off, but I'm afraid it's not so logical as that." Dr. Marschdin held up an empty suit coat, a tie wrapped around the collar, a dress shirt beneath it. "These were his clothes, the very clothes he was wearing when he literally vanished before my eyes.

"Friends, there is a reason I refer to the pathologist as only 'the pathologist'. I haven't the faintest idea what his true name is or was, if he is lost to us. It has completely abandoned my memory. I can only wonder if it was ever in there at all. But I do doubt myself, as there is in our profession plenty of room for doubt. Science, in particular, asks us to consider what yesterday we took for truth as today's superstition. Even these clothes, there's no telling whom they belonged to, and I might have imagined that the whole thing occurred. Why, it's possible that the entirety of what I've now divulged is a hallucination set in the confines of my own imagination, part of some unfortunate psychotic episode I'm now enduring, unbeknownst to my unconscious self. For all I know, our pathologist was never an inhabitant of our world, but only of my mind. There is hope yet so take heart. If the pathologist doesn't exist, it stands to reason that the very thing he studied does not exist, either. Imagine that those afflicted are now free of their suffering. *There is no disease. There is nothing to cure.* Say it with me now, folks."

And everyone began to repeat what Dr. Marschdin said, without aping the labored and nasally intonation of his voice, "There is no disease. There is nothing to cure."

I knew this, as answer to my illness, would not do. I was still very sick and becoming sicker. I had only one option. I raced to the stage, as quickly as my enfeebled, wrecked body could move. Dr. Marschdin saw me out of his periphery, and his eyes became wide. He recognized that I was one of the ill. I was one of the people looking for answers. He reached out to embrace me. He assumed I was pleased with him, with everything. Freedom, that's what had happened. As if the pathologist had caused my illness for the simple fact of desiring its cure.

I punched Dr. Marschdin square in the jaw, leveling him.

Now that he was on the floor, completely dazed and defenseless, I really thrashed him. I grabbed his coat by the lapel with one hand and continued to unload haymaker after haymaker, destroying his glasses and knocking him out. The rest of the people in attendance were stunned and didn't react. Some, though, very few mind you, but still some, cheered me on as I continued my thrashing.

Dr. Marschdin is now in a medically induced coma while they endeavor to treat his injury, his damaged and swollen brain. No one doubts *his* injury's existence.

I'm meanwhile left in chains, still very sick but now also incarcerated. I've been attempting to send letters indicating my predicament to the pathologist, but they've all been returned to me, unopened. *NO ONE BY THAT NAME EXISTS; GET OVER*

IT is stamped in red to each envelope.

The guards laugh at me. I understand. They've been trained to feel no pity for people like myself, people who live in these cages. It still doesn't excuse the guards for having one among them pretend to be "the pathologist" and then for the rest of them to come climbing out of the shadows and reveal their lies at the last moment, right when finally I think I'll be cured. I am guilty of falling for their trick every time.

I will continue to be tricked, for as long as I remain alive and able. There is the possibility that the pathologist could return. He could be out there right now, waiting to bring me back to wellness. He might even restore me to a life worth living. It is possible. I have every reason to believe it is possible.

the walk-in-their footsteps historical footsteps museum

There are a lot more dead raccoons in the roads and along the roadsides lately.

I mention the raccoons because while I am driving they are what I am sometimes seeing. It is sad to see many of anything dead, even raccoons, whom some people regard as pests. I know for a fact that some people regard raccoons as pests because I said to my neighbor Bill: "Hey Bill, have you seen there's all these dead raccoons on the roads and by the sides of roads these days?" And all he said in reply—which was almost inaudible because of the low, gravelly-throated sound his voice naturally makes, and because he wasn't looking directly at me out of apparent indifference—was that it was a good thing they were dead, because it kept them "*out* of his trash cans and *in* hell."

He added that he might have killed them himself with his Ford F-150, which he drove recklessly on both dirt and paved roads. And he smiled this sort of horrifying smile that prompted me to just finish the conversation altogether by saying, "Oh, well good-bye." I walked quickly into my home, wherein I locked the door hurriedly and only partly out of habit.

I'm not in a good place with all the dead raccoons, regardless of Bill. I only wish there weren't so many dead, and not just for the obvious sanitation issues their decomposing carcasses create.

❋

Business has been picking up at my job, big time. My job is mostly head custodian at the Walk-in-Their-Footsteps Histori-cal Footsteps Museum. We're a for-profit museum run by private interests. Does that qualify us as a museum, technically speak-ing? I am not clear on this. Apparently the answer's *yes*, though, because we have not been shut down or censured, to my knowl-edge, and business is booming. And also consider that my own circumstances as head custodian have improved mightily over the last several weeks as a result of this business boom.

I've simultaneously moved into the position of walking in foot-steps, much as footstep-walking predecessors once did, with just the same amount of skill and enthusiasm. And I will get to how that came to pass in short order.

Betsy, who works for the museum as both the ticket vendor in the box office and as a cashier in the gift shop, was the first to let me know we've got a salable tour show all of a sudden—and she would know. She sells the tickets and merchandise. She can see whether they are going like hotcakes. "That's how they're going," she told me.

But let me explain to you exactly what is the now-salable Walk-in-Their-Footsteps Historical Footsteps Museum and its now-salable tour show—*tour show* is what we officially call it, for legality concerns most likely.

Mr. and Mrs. Dabler are the owners and the founders. The idea for the museum itself came about when—to paraphrase her own account—Mrs. Janice Dabler was at home one evening, thinking *and* walking around in her kitchen, a hand clasped to a wide cylindrical glass of red wine, and she realized out of nowhere, as if thought-struck, that all historical figures had to "tread turf" (her words) across somewhere in their lifetimes. She imagined they were real and as alive as she was at one historical epoch or another, walking around in their kitchens and drinking wines and such themselves, probably—except perhaps drinking from goblets or chalices instead of JC Penney glassware.

Mrs. Dabler then explained to her husband this thought about historical figures and their footsteps. Caleb Dabler, her husband, raised a not-ironical eyebrow. It occurred to him that she might really be onto something good, money-wise. He immediately thought of General George A. Custer, because of Custer's Last Stand, which I gather Caleb sort of misinterpreted as referring to where Custer was literally standing when he died, and what precise number that *stand* represented in relation to the total sequential number of *stands* he'd experienced during his relatively short lifetime of 36 years. Which is a somewhat thoughtful thought.

A brief aside about Caleb: he once told me when I started working for him, "You won't exactly be working for peanuts," he said, "but then you won't exactly be working for eagles, either.

Maybe *some*day you will, but not *to*day, Ed." My name, by the way, is Edward "Ed" Bryson, which explains Caleb's calling me that. And it turns out that to him eagles are representative of an enormous sum of monetary payment, as essentially the opposite of working for peanuts. That's just Caleb's way, though, making up phrases and words and saying strange things that have got possibly coded meaning or not. He never explains. Another time he asked me in a serious tone of voice if my "rhino cherry" was working all right, and I *still* don't fully understand what he meant by that.

I wasn't working for eagles then, or even at the start of our business' boom. "These things take time," the Dablers explained. "Sure do," they added.

᠅

OK, so speaking of the Walk-in-Their-Footsteps Historical Footsteps Museum, which is located at approximately Rapid City, South Dakota, which is where I live, also, basically; they built it in this sort of obscure rural location that's a little bit hard to get to by automobile (horse is a different matter), but you can find it taking Highway 16 south out of Rapid City. It's at about the halfway point between Rapid City and Mt. Rushmore. There's a big billboard a few miles ahead of the museum's exit that's got a picture of cartoon versions of General George A. Custer and Gutzon Borglum (the sculptor who designed and built Mt. Rushmore), who are essentially drawn walking normally enough but for that each has an arm locked over the shoulder of the other, and each has a leg kicked forward in the exaggerated style of The Rockettes. Their faces are smiling like a Teddy Roosevelt caricature, big and toothy. Plus for a real humor element, they are following after a scrambling, crazy-legged Crazy Horse, who is sending up billowing clouds of smoke and debris with the frantic movement of his speedy "crazy" legs, and who it seems in the illustration on the billboard is mostly just trying to get away, similar to a female cat mistaken for a female skunk by the Looney Toons' Pepe Le Pew.

The billboard advertises The Walk-in-Their-Footsteps Historical Footsteps Museum in red bubble letters, which are readable but somewhat squished together, as bubble letters are known for being. We're also featured in several pamphlets we pay to have distributed at various hotels and restaurants in the Rapid City area.

And once off the highway exit ramp, not too far past the Mobil gas station and the not-much-else there is around it, you have to travel down this dirt road (which I've heard reminds people of the classic novel and better-remembered film *Deliverance*, which that did hurt our popularity up until recently, when we got popular and business began to boom, and people no longer cared how out in the sticks we were). The dirt road leads up to what turns into a gravel parking lot of white pebbles and stones, a pale-ish aggregate of assorted light-to-deep shades, extending in what I see as a pond-shaped circle in front of the museum's entrance. Concrete stairs and a very recently added concrete ramp for the disabled lead up to the entrance.

The museum on the whole is massive, and looks a lot like three stacked toy blocks of successively greater size, with the smallest block on top and so on down. The building is sky blue and made of brick, and it has in contrast a darker shade of blue, the color of a Navy service uniform, coating its mansard roof. Mansard roofing surrounds each block floor with the next floor ascending above it, except the top floor of course, which is only mansard roof and has no additional floor above it, naturally. There are some air-conditioning units up there, though, but those are not at all visible from below.

Dressing the mansard roofing at each level around the non-slanted edges is spear-pointed, wrought-iron balustrade. They look like small fences. And so, to complete it with our own special touch, welded to the center of the many crossed bars are the metallic outlines of variously sized shapes of feet, walking across the balustrade like they, the historical figures who walked, had defied gravity and left their footprints up there permanently for every tourist to see and, if they feel the urge, remark about excitedly, and purchase pictures of themselves near to. There's a small balcony on the second floor that allows you access to the lower floor's balustrade and photo opportunities for only a nominal fee.

❉

It's inside this very blue building that you take your tour show, costing twenty dollars for adults (everyone thirteen and older, that is), half that for students and seniors, eight dollars for children six to twelve, and nothing for children under the age of five, which I think is a pretty nice deal. The tour show originally, in a nutshell, consisted of reasonably similar-looking wooden facsimiles of various famous people walking in lines of footprints we purport they once "walked in." But it's definitely not even certain that Custer was ever literally walking where his alleged footprints have placed him inside the museum. The facsimiles were shoddy enough to rouse several complaints from customers (the few we had then), most of which had to do with the fact that it is misleading to say famous people have ever actually walked here inside the museum (or even on the soil that existed at this location before the museum was built over it), and that they, the customers, are thus allowed to literally step on (or walk in) the footprints (or footsteps) ascribed to whichever historical figure (Another aside: to be clear we let the customers walk in the footsteps of each historical person on display, and at that time—when the historical figures were made of wood—we allowed the customers to walk in footsteps up to the point just before they'd bump into the facsimile, which obviously didn't itself move but was instead mannequin inert, and the facsimiles were very fragile as an added negative), but back to the specific footprints, we have had some customers who are very dissatisfied because they are dubious, not unreasonably, of whether we have on display genuine historical footsteps, which is what our pamphlet claims we do, sort of.

But as Caleb or Janice, or sometimes Betsy, has to deftly explain to angry patrons, there is a tiny star or asterisk—I forget which it is exactly—next to the wording in the pamphlet that claims historical figures have actually stepped foot on the actual floor inside our museum. And if you follow that tiny star to its corresponding tiny star on the bottom of the page and you read the adjacent fine print, you will see that it goes on to elaborate somewhat convolutedly the following:

> *i.e., just as in any hypothetical scenario you yourself might think up, we here at the Walk-in-Their-Footsteps Historical Footsteps Museum have imagined anyone living or dead is or was capable of having hypothetically walked anywhere on Earth without it really ever being recorded. The Walk-in-Their-Footsteps Museum makes no claim to possess definitive proof of famous individuals having ever, beyond all doubt, stepped in the building known as the Walk-in-Their-Footsteps Museum. We merely suggest the*

possibility that such was perhaps the case with respect to our museum and the exhibits of suggested historical footsteps herein. The Walk-in-Their-Footsteps Historical Footsteps Museum offers no refunds to customers regarding this or any other misunderstanding having to do with our tour show. Don't forget to visit our gift shop where supplies of walking historical figures, complete with—for a small additional fee—Walk-in-Their-Footsteps miniaturized walking sticks, are limited.

And this assertion is also written in tiny print on all tickets and above the box office beneath the big red and white sign that reads: TICKETS. This has protected us from legal action and having to give money back, but at the time of the wooden facsimiles it only served to hurt our reputation as what was already considered a lower-end sort of tourist trap. Business, as already said, has been picking up real quick, which has a lot to do with the actor Caleb hired to play General George A. Custer. Because another valid complaint of our customers was that basically we were offering a much, much crappier version of any of the thousands of terrible-to-mediocre wax museums that litter the American tourist-trap-scape. At least even the worst wax figures came close to resembling human beings. This was not true of our wooden facsimiles, which more closely resembled deformed scarecrows.

I mean, you kind of assume that replacing a wooden, only serviceable facsimile of General George Armstrong Custer with a flesh and blood honest-to-God human being is going to have a positive net effect on your dismal reputation, but to say that about Neal Send, who was the actor hired by Caleb to play Custer, would be a total understatement. The Neal Send effect was way more sweeping than just replacing wood with human. It's the first thing that allowed business to boom.

Neal sort of came in on the wind, and his hiring wasn't totally an accident, but wasn't totally on purpose, either. I heard what happened was Neal stood next to the wooden Custer facsimile one day, and when people would walk by on their tour shows, he spoke imploringly to them, unabashedly dismissing the value of the wooden facsimile, "I look more like Custer than this. Right folks? Mm-i-right?" He gestured with his hand flat and horizontal, holding it up beneath the block of wood's crummy face and then to his not-crummy and actually almost handsome face. The audience was left to decide. Some replied aloud that he did indeed look more like Custer, from what they knew of the historical man. Caleb and security were summoned eventually. And of course at first Caleb seemed ready to unleash the hounds of litigation against Neal, but he kept scrutinizing Neal's features. Finally, like pretty much everyone else in the audience, he came to agree with Neal. And that was enough for Caleb to think maybe Neal would be better for business than a wooden facsimile.

Neal's success prompted Caleb and Janice to hire other actors to play the roles of various historical figures such as Gutzon Borglum, Crazy "Legs" Horse (the roadrunner legs image has stuck and become a popular nickname, which certain people consider insensitive – but lots of things are, these days), Abraham Lincoln, Mark Twain, and Mohandas Gandhi, who is the only one I'm near positive never stepped foot on the interior of U.S. America's mainland, much less as far northwest as South Dakota and the greater Rapid City area.

Neal insisted on being called "Georgie" or "Custy" when he was in character. So that's basically what I knew him as, "Custy." I was just "Ed" to him, because all I did was mop the floors and see about general repairs and clean up after the filthy kids who do disgusting things in the bathroom, which their parents leave for me to just sort of deal with, saying effectively, "You deal."

Custy could also juggle, and so when he'd regale the audience with his smooth way of walking in his character's own supposed footsteps, he'd also juggle and then real fluidly do a backflip and a hand stand. Custy was really nimble, too, and acrobatic. He called that part of the tour show his "The Amazing Custy Show," and the customers took notice. Caleb and Janice eagerly approved his segment's name change, and began to advertise it as such in a new version of the pamphlet. The new version had a cannily lit cover photo of Custy flipping in midair, to the smiling approval of the barely visible spectators (you could just barely perceive their white-toothed grins). And regarding Neal's great success as Georgie Custy, Caleb went so far as to say, "I may not know about General Custer, but that man is Custer as far as I'm concerned. And it won't be long now before he's making the big eagles—for us *and* for him, that is."

✳

People flocked to walk in the historical footsteps of Neal as Georgie "Custy" Custer, the general. They filled in the expansive blue rooms vacant of any old-timey set props (it was pretty much just Neal out there as Custy). Custy would run out into the center of the action and the people were corralled outside of his show part of the tour show by velvet rope guardrails and signs imploring them not to enter Custy's circle while he is walking and cartwheeling in his own footsteps. The crowd applauded mightily at his every amusing gesture and feat of physical derring-do. Custy would sometimes stroke his mustache and wonder aloud,

"Where will history lead me, to fortune and greater fame having nothing to do with a hubris-driven and violent, untimely demise?" The dramatic irony of such a question was not lost on the crowd, some of the youngest and most historically aware among them shouted *Nooooo, no, nooo, noooo!* in a keyed-up, emphatic tone, like the studio audience of a children's television show. And throughout all of this Neal's adroit showmanship and plentiful charisma were on display for spectators to view and get lost in. Which believe you me, they always did.

The other actors weren't and aren't nearly as good as Neal. They're fine and all, but Neal was the total and complete heart of our initial success, vitally pumping our tour show to local renown. Which is why it was a pretty big deal when he had a kind of meltdown not very long ago and said he was through with the tour show altogether. Caleb wanted to talk about it with me, seeing as I had the closest thing to a friendship with him of anybody at the museum.

I went to Caleb's office, and we talked about the situation, Caleb and I.

"OK, so sit down a minute and let me tell you this is not good, this…is…not…good," Caleb said, shaking his head as if all was lost. "I'm thinking finally the Lord has seen fit to bless me with a brilliant draw, and then the draw turns around and says he ain't working anymore. And this is gonna cost everybody, you, me, Neal, and everybody. But, mind you, Neal doesn't seem to care. Which is awfully selfish of him."

Caleb was chomping a cigar angrily with his back molars, sort of gritting his teeth with it, like you'd stereotypically expect of wealthy bigwigs as they carry out the business of the day with this severe importance. I think the money and the power that comes with running a reasonably successful attraction in a somewhat highly trafficked tourist destination such as Rapid City has gone to his head a little, but I didn't say that, especially not then. I was definitely unconvinced I could be of much help, too. By this time Neal had been working for us for a while, and I had developed a relationship of workplace sociability with him, but I wouldn't have considered myself his friend. I wasn't most people's friend.

"Well what do you want me to do about it?" I said.

"I dunno, couldn't you maybe talk some sense into him? The guy's clearly gone off his rocker. He's got no dice in those gears anymore. Get him his dice back, so his gears start going again," Caleb said, losing aplomb in his speech with each passing ludicrously mixed metaphor. "He'll maybe acknowledge you when you talk to him, which is more than what I got, which was complete nothingness. Somebody turn back time to the time of lights being on and not off."

"Where is he? Is he still around someplace, like in here?"

"Like in where? This office? Do you see him at all anywhere in here?"

"In the building, I mean," I said, although actually I *had* meant in Caleb's office someplace, for example, perhaps he was inside Caleb's closet, but really that still doesn't make much sense.

"Nah, he's outside on that hill. That's where he's been most of the day. I think talking to himself. And, anyway, he's not doing a whole lot that's good for business. I'll just say that about what he's doing."

Caleb gestured towards the window with this dismissive jerk of his thumb. I scanned the landscape outside, and I could make out Neal on the hill next to the Footsteps Museum. He was seated in a crouching position. His knees were pressed up against his chest and he had his arms securely wrapped around his legs as if to hug himself. He rocked back and forth in the wind's languid caress, seeking calm and serenity. I am unsure of whether the dull force of the wind was rocking his body or if it was just he alone who was rocking himself. The sky was shiny with blue, which enveloped the museum a bit, as it was something close to the same shiny sky color and the patter of birds hitting windows and walls seemed constant.

"So if he's through with the whole thing, why's he still here?"

"That's what I'm saying. I said to Janice, I said: 'We've got a grain of tiny hope seeing as he hasn't yet left for greener pastures of the bright neon lights of Broadway Street.' Naturally, she was in full agreement. She said to get you, which I did." Caleb assumed the proud expression of a boy who'd done right by his mother, a good boy, which was kind of their relationship, a little bit odd though it was.

"All right, well, I guess I'll go visit with him, then."

"Good," he said. "Oh, and Ed?"

"Yeah?"

"How's your rhino cherry doin'?" Caleb asked this very sincerely.

✼

I walked up the hill to be with Neal, to see what the heck was up. And when I got there, he had not moved from the self-hugging position I'd seen him in from Caleb's office.

"What's this all about, Neal. Or, uh, Custy?"

He stared ahead thoughtfully, apparently trying to decide whether I was someone he was willing to talk to, and then after a moment he decided that I was, "No, I'm Neal. Just Neal. It's all I ever was. Never was I Custy, not really."

"Well, then, Neal, Mr. and Mrs. Dabler and everybody's awful worried about you, and so am I, I guess. They thought, and so did

I, that I should see about your health and all that. Is everything good? I mean, obviously it's not, but why is it exactly that it's not good? People only want to help you, myself included. I'm here to help."

Neal looked up, at last. His face was flush. He looked sickly with hay fever or some other allergic reaction to the pollens and other organic debris sent swirling around by the dull breeze.

"It's that I'm a fraud, Ed. It's that who could be proud of me? Not the woman of my dreams. Not her. She doesn't even know me!"

"Aww, it can't be as bad as all that. So this is about a woman, then?" Suddenly I thought I understood Neal's predicament and could be of real help. "So she's gonna like you better somehow if you just let your life go to hell and do nothing?"

Neal gripped his chin hard, tilting his head towards the ground in what looked like he was caught in sudden, deep deliberation.

"Well, no, it's not like that, really. See, I mean, she's a girl I used to know, ok? And I went to her house the other day, after probably about a decade or two of not seeing her or speaking a word to her in email, letter, or over the phone, etc. You get the idea. I told her that I'm a famous George Armstrong Custer reenactor at the Walk-in-Their-Footsteps Historical Footsteps Museum. I had the whole outfit and mustache on and everything. She said, 'Who?' and then, after I showed her some identification and some pictures taken of us together in our youth, she said, 'Where have you been for the last over two decades?' And I told her, plain and simple: 'I'd been pining for you,' meaning her, 'from afar.' Eh, not you as in *you*, Ed."

"I assumed, and I am OK with that," I said.

"Good, so yeah. She was not won over by my declaration of my love for her from afar these many years. She said she's sorry but she plans to marry this other guy, her fiancé. His name is

Tucker or something. She loves him and stuff. And anyway, she says, what kind of nerve do I have coming out of nowhere after being her friend from childhood and nothing else? And now I'm back here saying I love her and want to, what's more, propose marriage (which I did do that, too, Ed)? She says, 'Hey, no way, buddy. I've got my own life to lead, and I'm leading it with Tucker, and don't be so weird anymore,' because I'd apparently totally freaked her out."

"I guess I can't say I blame her, Neal. I'm sorry but I can't. That is pretty weird to do."

"Yeah, and it gets worse. Because I was looking at it like it was this movie scene. I think that was partly the problem, see? I'd gotten lost in the fantasy of it. Like the anticipation of being with her seemed better than the actually being with her, after a while. Which is why it probably took me so long to re-insinuate myself into her life. But so, I told her, like it was a movie, 'Don't walk out on me, Camille (her name's Camille, by the way). You walk out on me and you'll be making the worst decision of your life, you hear me? The worst decision of your life! We are only complete when we are whole and together!' To which she just rolled her eyes and closed the door on me. When I wouldn't leave her porch, she called the cops. Then I ran. And that was it, for now at least."

He paused, started picking at some grass and threw the blades up above his head and sprinkle the ground. He didn't seem completely insane, although his story was pretty much that. I thought of poking him to see if he was real. But then I thought doing that would probably itself seem a little insane.

"That should probably be it forever," I said, as discouragingly as I could manage while still sounding encouraging in another way, a way having less to do with his interest in Camille, or so I hoped it sounded to him.

Neal wasn't listening and went on, "I got home and took one of my 'long showers.'" He air-quoted "long showers" with the two fingers of each of his two hands, whatever his doing so was intended to signify. "And when I got out I had this melancholy feeling like what is the point of going on like this? What was I doing and why? I'm not George A. Custer, and I'm never going to be."

"Yeah. I mean, right? What, did you think you were actually Custy himself, Neal? You didn't think that."

"In a way, completely, I did. I walked in his footsteps, didn't I? If I'm not him, then nobody is. And I'm not him."

"No, you aren't him, Neal. You're Neal Send. That's who you are."

"Nah, that's not true. *Neal* isn't even my real name, truth be told," He air-quoted Neal, too. The air-quotes were starting to get annoying.

"Uh, huh," I said, not sure of really how to handle Neal not being Neal but a stranger basically to me. We weren't even close to begin with. "So who are you, then? If not Neal."

"I told you, Ed. I was Custy. I was really him, I think. I don't have anybody to be anymore. I don't know who I am. I probably never did."

"That's a real pickle."

"I'll say," a man who was not named Neal, I guess, said.

❋

I returned and reported what I'd learned to Caleb, who was obviously not very happy about his tour show's star's sudden fall from reality, if that's what it was that he fell from, and possibly sanity.

"Oh god, what the hell? Damn it! Every time! Every time I think, hey God's shining some of that happiness and yellow on me that others enjoy, He goes and He says, 'Sorry Caleb Dabler, but you are not one of my chosen few. No sir.'"

Caleb was chewing on the nub of his cigar as if it were the cuticle of his thumb or index finger, rendering his cigar unmanageably deformed. The back end had been pulled apart by his biting and was spilling its dried tobacco leaves into his mouth, the taste of which caused him to cringe. Refusing to be daunted, though, he continued smoking in vain, as he was visibly unwilling to concede another point to his suddenly un-loving god.

"I don't know what to do about Neal or whoever he is," Janice said, sitting in on our meeting this time, as things had worsened noticeably to everyone's visible dismay. "But we've got to let the tour show go on. We need a George A. Custer replacement for until Neal is back to his less batshit self. We are so completely desperate for somebody, for *a body.*" She looked at me, so did Caleb.

"Hey, don't look at me. I'm just the head janitor remember? What do I know about any of this? I'm no showman is all."

"You're the *only* janitor," Caleb said, gagging and then pausing to wipe the tobacco leaves from his now dangling tongue with his handkerchief. "By default I guess that makes you the *head* janitor, but I don't know. Listen, though, you said you always wanted to work for eagles. Well this is how you make the big bucks with the huge ass antlers capable of destroying their buck adversaries, get me?"

"Not by being the 'head' janitor will you have this chance, Ed," Janice averred.

I thought about it long and hard, probably not long and hard, enough, but still pretty long and pretty hard. And while I worried what replacing "Neal" as Custy would do to "Neal"'s fragile psyche, I also realized well enough that if I ever wanted to make the eagles Caleb talked about, this'd be my only chance. I wasn't totally sure I wanted to make the eagles Caleb talked about, but I'm pretty easy to convince.

So I acquiesced and took the role, and I remained the head janitor, too, with the full title of *head janitor* and everything. I decided also I couldn't be any worse than the other actors we had on staff, especially Gandhi, who was and still is played by this septuagenarian erstwhile auto mechanic, a grizzled, old white man who refuses to wear any makeup whatsoever and will slip out of character and say offensive things all the time, but nobody visiting seems to care or pay attention much to Gandhi, the historical figure, a man I guess most people traveling in these parts are only faintly aware actually in real life existed, and so our actor's missteps never matter much. Our Gandhi is also not very good at walking in his historical footsteps. He has an uncomfortable habit of losing his head, like a robot rebooting, and slamming face-first to the floor, whereon prostrate and motionless, he apparently waits for someone to come and correct the problem of his planting himself there face down. Heavy past and present methamphetamine use may play a part in the actor's erratic, drugged-up behavior, but honestly I'm not sure. We're not really on speaking terms.

And although verisimilitude never seemed to matter much to "Neal" and the Dablers, I went to great lengths to ensure that I looked like the genuine article, 100% the same as "Neal" dressed as Georgie "Custy" Custer, the general. I did pretty well with the suspenders and the orange boots "Neal" would wear and back-flip in nimbly. His purple shoelaces were harder to come by, but eventually I found a pair. I had a pretty poorly kept beard going before all the stuff occurred, and so I tried to refashion it to look more like Custy, which was hard because it was extremely thin and adolescent-looking. But I wasn't embarrassed enough by the end result of my creative shaving to abandon the whole enterprise in favor of a fake mustache.

*

I made my debut the next day. There was a large crowd assembled, as Caleb had sent word to two local radio stations that the star of the Walk-in-Their-Footsteps Historical Footsteps Museum tour show had basically returned and the tour show was to go on as scheduled. The radio stations were paid to mention this. So it was advertising really, I guess, on the radio. It was a paid-for radio advertisement.

"Neal" was watching me with eyes that said *no* really sadly. His *no* wasn't like a no of admonition, but a no that was like pleading with me diffidently. I tried hard not to concentrate on "Neal" after that, and was largely successful.

Caleb had rigged these pyrotechnics of lesser quality to detonate upon my entrance and distract from my part of the tour show, for fear I wasn't up to the task of filling "Neal"'s orange Custy boots. I thought the pyrotechnics were probably a bad idea considering it was a pretty enclosed space to be setting off pyrotechnics and there was no fire marshal on hand to ensure it was all up to code and, most importantly, safe for the kids. So that wasn't a great idea from my point of view, but I didn't argue with Caleb.

"I hope this doesn't go horribly awry," Caleb said. "From the very bottom of my heart I hope that. In the way of expectations I have for you, Ed, do not worry, there are none. Just go out there and survive and, hell, maybe you'll do the job so badly that whatever-his-name-is will come back to us with both arms open, completely desirous of ending the madness you've wrought with your crummy excuse of a Custer. But till he does exactly that we can't have anyone who's not up to the task of walking in Custer's footsteps, so I hope you are and that's it. That's all I have to say. I hope I've been helpful, but it's not my fault if I haven't."

I was trying desperately—apart from Caleb's chattering—to channel a mindset different from my own. I didn't even care if I resembled "Neal" or Custy in the slightest. I just needed to be somebody with a little bravado, or having more than the basically none that I possessed.

But there I stood, in my awkward-fitting western cavalry officer's replica uniform, epaulets of green and purple with sparkling glitter. I balled my fists in black and white chessboard-patterned gloves. There was a patch of adhesive set on the palm of each glove to help me *stick* my various acrobatic landings, something I was not very sure of, sticking landings. Caleb's inspired festive atmosphere and his DJ-at-a-high-school-prom heralding through reverb-flooded microphone of the return of Custy to the museum were building the crowd's expectations to an impossibly feverous pitch. I listened in and waited for my cue as I strained behind the white curtain to get my balled fists unstuck. My cue was unfortunately the firing of the pyrotechnics.

Caleb fired them off, of which he had around seven or fewer rockets, and I think he did it a little prematurely, although I was prepared for something to go wrong with them. I did not anticipate a spent lift charge casing arcing and caroming off of the 30-foot ceiling and then from which point proceeding to careen downwardly at its new trajectory to where it finally touched down at a high velocity directly between my eyes. I mean it touched down hard. I felt a welt beginning to form, one that no doubt would make me look all the more clownish to the spectators. So this disoriented me enough not to notice a young prankster girl in pigtails had moved the velvet rope directly in my way, in the short distance between the white curtain and Custy's footsteps.

And though I'd been hit in the face and welted, I'd managed to keep running towards the audience, carrying a large old-timey American flag with one hand over my shoulder.

My speed and disorientation were working in equal parts against me, so that I then caught both of my feet on the velvet rope as I leapt to do a cartwheel (the only semi-acrobatic move I came close to perfecting during my trial runs—or walks—the evening before). The flag was sent through the air like a javelin, but I think it got lodged safely in the drywall, thankfully not touching the ground, which would have been the real tragedy. Like my friend Gandhi, I tripped ridiculously and planted my face smack dab in the middle of the line of Custy's footsteps. The audience, shielding its collective self from the onslaught of seven fireworks' debris seconds earlier, was at first taken aback by my thorough and booming plunge and then amused to the point of a one-year-old child at the disastrous spectacle I'd made of myself, crying out altogether in mirth-filled ecstasy. I managed to stagger upwardly to a standing-like position, and Caleb pantomimed that I should keep it going, that in effect the show must go on. I smiled with broken teeth and bowed for a second, removing my oversized Styrofoam cowboy hat, which was the best we could do for headwear on such short notice. Then it becomes a little sketchy for me, because, I later would learn from Rapid City Regional Hospital staff, I bruised my brain fairly well and was for that infirmity slower to recover my senses in the wake of my fall.

From what I hear of the events that unfolded following my bow, the short of it is that I clownishly continued to great avail to endear myself to the crowd, who by the end of the tour show had assumedly forgotten all about "Neal" and were chanting for Georgie A. Custy (i.e., me), as if I were now the general himself. Eventually Caleb decided I'd walked in Custer's footsteps for long enough like an automaton, and so he called for a stretcher and the stretcher and its complement of paramedics finally carted me away to the near-riotous protests of the tour show-goers, who then descended into actual riot beyond anyone's control, and flipped over several cars in the parking lot and started small fires that eventually became one big fire. Caleb and Janice were not thrilled about the damage but appreciative for all the free press the ensuing violence and mayhem garnered from the national media. There were even helicopters. The Dablers later sent Nancy Grace a beautiful bouquet of professionally ornamented footsteps made of colored paper-and-cardboard-mache.

While I was in the hospital for observation over the next day, Janice sent me a ten-dollar bottle of Shiraz, which was for the most part full, and a "get well" card demanding my imminent recovery and return to work, reminding me of my very limited health insurance coverage. Basically it just said, "Come back real soon, or else you'll be severed and we'll find someone new." This filled my recovering brain with thoughts of dread, but I calmed it and the rest of my anesthetized-feeling body by the realization that they must be encouraged by my performance and eagerly anticipating my return, if they're willing to debase themselves like this to a lowly head janitor. And that made a lot of sense to my recovering brain.

The hardest part of my job now is creating new and inventive ways to fall. My body can take it. I have a lot of thick calluses to pad me. But the crowd is fickle. They don't want to see the same man tripping over the same velvet rope week in and week out. The first new idea I had was to place a ladder in the path of

Custer's footsteps. In order to continue on my way, I'd need to climb the ladder and then jump down from it, landing in whatever way fate decides.

"Neal" left the tour show for good following my rise to stardom, but before he left Rapid City, he went to the courthouse and had his name legally changed to Neal Send, so now wherever he went, he'd just be Neal Send. No more hiding behind a mysterious identity.

And recently I realized that I'm now the reason business is booming. Isn't that great for me?

Neal was the reason business boomed at first, but Neal is gone, and in his footsteps I now walk.

new slim

Slim wasn't the same *Slim* after teleporting from one side of the living room to the other, inside his teleportation machine. Something in his walk, about his walk, that he seemed to walk more than he once did, even, was different, was apart from what he and his walk used to be.

Slim used to enjoy playing checkers, but New Slim did not. Slim never asked to be called *New Slim*, and I wouldn't imagine the old Slim would see any reason to refer to himself differently, using a *new* name, even, if he were the same old Slim.

New Slim wanted me to know how different he was, but he said I shouldn't think it's weird. And maybe, he'd suggest real casually,

I should go through the teleportation machine—not because it would make me a new person, as though this were *Invasion of the Body Snatchers* or something, and the person coming out of the machine would be a copy of me but physically not me—but instead because it's a rush to go through the machine and I might enjoy it and I probably wouldn't even call myself *New Rich* afterwards, as though I were different from the Rich I understood myself to be at the present time. I'd most likely be the Rich I've always been, and understand myself to be such.

He said this in a way that reminded me of how kids will hide things in plain sight, like if they have a cookie or gum or something they're not supposed to have. Sooner or later you get them to reveal that mashed-up mound of whatever they were hiding in the palm of their gross hand, though. I got the impression it would be that way with New Slim, likewise. I was worried it would be, in metaphor, exactly as horrible as I suspected—a crushed chocolate bar gooey with caramel. Disgusting sticky crap all over that hand.

"I'm just going to teleport the plants and the pets through the teleportation machine. Nothing worthy of arousing suspicions," New Slim said, teleporting those things. They came out the other side indefinably different, too, though he went to great pains to emphasize that it was simply another coincidence.

I couldn't be OK with it. Dogs barked differently. Cats meowed differently. Plants existed differently. And they all seemed to be attempting to coax me into The Machine.

The apartment was soon populated by slightly different teleported creatures and items. Without being able to grasp why or how, I never felt at home after that. New Slim was always either watching the New TV or doing pull-ups, which was something Old Slim would never do. Old Slim was not very interested in exercise. Old Slim preferred to drink beer and curse and spit and order things off of the internet.

New Slim watched strange new television programs on the new TV, too. So did the other living creatures in the apartment, the new dogs, cats, lizards, parrots, turtles, and all of them. The news on that television was strange. The newscaster's hair was odd, and his face seemed to be made of plaster, falling apart on screen.

"What you said about everything and the teleportation machine isn't true," I told New Slim.

He had to have known I'd confront him eventually. He didn't seem at all surprised by what I'd said.

"Can't you see I'm trying to watch the new television?" he replied. "One of us cares about current events, and one of us is preoccupied with a delusion. I've moved passed this discussion. It's done. I'm over it."

"You are not who you used to be. You've changed, man. You're an entirely changed man," I said, waving a cast iron frying pan in an aggressive, twirling motion. (And don't think for a second that the idea of the pan going through the teleportation machine didn't run through my mind, making me suspect it was not a weapon I could rely on. I was well aware of that prospect.)

"If anyone's changed, it's you. I'm the same. I haven't changed. I've been who I am for as long as I can remember. Aren't you worried you might be getting paranoid? The Rich I used to know was never paranoid. But are *you* Old Rich?" His words stung. That was exactly what made New Slim hard to deal with—he spotted my areas of insecurity and brutalized them. Not that I hadn't made it easy for him. I'd broadcasted my insecurities loudly, sure, but New Slim was always ready to dig in.

I freaked out over the thought of myself as an infant. I recall an episode at the age of ten or so, buried deep in the recesses of my mind, precipitated by my mother showing me pictures of myself when I couldn't have been older than four, or maybe six. I reacted to those pictures with horror. I remembered how I responded with a few brief shrieks and then a long while of paralytic shock, standing without movement, staring out into nothing. Disbelieving while having no choice but to believe, I was hearing the total truth from my mother.

It was me in the photograph, but it wasn't me—the blue jumper I was dressed in, a fuzzy black and white winter cap, a G.I. Joe action figure I must have lost long ago, a fairly new blanket that had since been reduced to tatters and typically crumpled throughout my adolescence in a pile at the foot of my bed, the latter's continued existence serving as further evidence of my mother's honesty. I was aware of how strange my reaction was, the way I responded to the images of myself—how in every way I could be told I was the person in those pictures—but I didn't remember any of it, a single second.

I've experienced the same horror at various times since, somewhat more lucid memories tenuously tying me to my more recent ages, but still so much that remains foggy and distant. I find myself experiencing the same muted horror as I believe I did when I was ten, looking at pictures of myself when I was four, or maybe six. That person was me, and now I'm someone else.

I'm uncomfortable being someone, having been someone else, always becoming someone new.

That still doesn't mean I don't have a good reason for not wanting to go into the teleportation machine. New Slim might have been *over it* but I wasn't.

So completely not *over it* was I that I went to work alerting the authorities. I told them about New Slim's machine, which they immediately didn't believe was real. I don't know why I expected any other reaction from them.

The truth means little in the grand scheme of things, especially when it concerns a machine that has never before existed in the whole of human history, a machine which people who aren't me have to take on faith does exist because I say it is so. This is not something people (the police especially) can normally afford to do. So I changed my story (not the most advisable next step when it comes to revealing things to the authorities, but I was weak and feeling I had no other options) and claimed our home had been burglarized, a thing that happens every day in the world. Two circumspect but wary police officers were at our door relatively quickly after that.

Unfortunately, all I'd done was lead the police right to New Slim, not the other way around. New Slim convinced them to try out his teleportation machine, The Machine, he called it. They both agreed to try it, which I found surprising, although the officers seemed to egg one another on and so in turn allayed each other's fears. Their normally skeptical and danger-detecting instincts were effectively numbed by New Slim. They ventured through time and space, or just one of those things, and came out the other side as though they were brand new to the world. They or *they* looked around and said, "There doesn't seem to be a problem here," in unison and were on their or *their* way. This was becoming a serious problem.

And my nights became fearful bouts of anticipating whether I would no longer be who I'd previously been or whether I had already happened and I *was* then different, changed in some indescribable way, left wondering if this fear was real fear or simply a vestige of the person I'd been. I didn't need to go through The Machine to know what it was capable of, just as I don't need to shed my own skin to know I'd react with horror if I ever did.

The police followed me to work, eyes aimed in my direction while they whispered secrets to each other like adolescents. They spoke with my boss, who shook his head at me while he listened.

Every time I convinced a police officer that I was telling the truth, he or she was brought back to the station for "Re-instruction" and lost to me. It appeared there were plenty of people who were willing to believe New Slim meant harm, but they were quickly gobbled up by The Machine. I avoided my apartment, but I saw an endless line of people going in and out of it. New Slim greeted them at the door and closed it behind them, suspicious of anyone who might be more curious than they ought to be.

I was still allowed to go inside my apartment. It was still the place in which I lived. New Slim lived there, too, but I still paid my half of the rent.

I took a baseball bat to The Machine and watched the springs and cogs and everything that makes The Machine a machine fly in all directions, metallic sounds ringing out with the constancy of music notes, The Machine broken beyond repair. I hoped New Slim wouldn't have the wherewithal to reconstruct it. It would have been nice if that knowledge was exclusive to Old Slim.

I expected to hear about what I'd done.

I did, soon. At work.

My boss asked if he could have a word with me.

"Hi Rich, bet you're wondering why I asked you in here, or perhaps you already have some idea. It's about The Machine, Slim's machine. You remember Slim, yeah? Your roommate." My boss asked this in a casual way, nothing like the boss I had hitherto known. There was nothing casual about my old boss. He was severe and formal, and he'd shown this with the bushy but well-groomed mustache he'd worn, which reminded me of a furrowed, angry eyebrow. My new boss, altered by The Machine, had shaved that mustache and started wearing sunglasses all the time, even indoors. He also kept a beard of finely manicured stubble. He looked like a young Kenny Loggins—a feature I'd never trusted in anyone. "We're going to ask that, from now on, you leave the machines that Slim builds alone."

He was so relaxed while he said this that I nearly didn't recognize I was being threatened. His pluralization of the word *machines*, likewise, unsettled me.

"How do you know I haven't changed, myself?" I asked. This wasn't just me playing games. I was genuinely hoping he'd have an answer.

"No one is saying that anyone has changed, Rich," my boss said. I could tell he was squinting despite his sunglasses. It was an irritated squint. "You seem awfully hung up on that idea, or so I've heard. Care to share why?"

"Because I'm losing sight of the things that matter. I can't get my footing. Have I gone through The Machine? Did it happen? Am I only continuing this pseudo-concern as a vestigial part of the consciousness that was copied and has now become my own?" I was flailing about, and my boss had already summoned the police to restrain me.

One police officer cuffed my hands behind my back, while another assisted him by pressing a nightstick against my throat and choking me momentarily. "Knock it off, will you?" the officer who'd choked me said, then struck me across the face with that same nightstick.

My boss stopped me as the police were leading me out of the building. I was apparently under arrest. "I wish you wouldn't be so obstinate, Rich. But then that's just like you. You've always been unwilling to see things any other way than the one you've already decided on. The world is everything you've decided is the case. This is what I've taken from seeing you behave the way you always have these past few years. I've always felt you were an asset to this company. I'm sorry to see you go."

We drove in a squad car for what felt like hours but couldn't possibly have been that long in actual fact. By the time we stopped, we'd only traveled halfway across town, judging by the few landmarks I recognized.

They took me to a small room in a library whose interior was built to resemble all of the grittiest neighborhoods of earlier iterations of New York City—somehow I was able to intuit this, no one explained this to me. We traveled down a narrow passage to the room in question, which was labeled G.I. Joe Headquarters and looked like the facade of an actual building all its own. I thought about how odd all of this was—that there remained no such organization as G.I. Joe.

Somewhat to my disappointment, that was precisely what I soon found out. This wasn't *G.I. Joe Headquarters* in any governmental sense, but it was the place, apparently, in which they designed all of Hasbro's variations of their G.I. Joe toys. This was the last place, naturally, I expected to find myself. But there I was. Men and women in white lab coats were huddled around me, asking me questions.

The Machine was still out there, New Slim pumping out new people and things and unleashing them on an unsuspecting planet, and all the while I was stuck in this place, answering the questions of action figure scientists. They were reminding me of a time in the past when I loved my G.I. Joes, how I would get up early on weekend mornings to play with the hundreds of them I'd acquired over the years, creating scenarios for them to be fighting to the very last man in my sister's doll house, which made an appropriate enough fortress for the bad guys.

"You feel your action figures' struggle now yourself, no? They fought to the last man and now you see yourself in a similar fight, correct?" The most stern of the action figure scientists asked. He appeared to be drawing something in a notebook, possibly a sketch for a new action figure. I worried what basis this had in my own life and present circumstances. How could any of what I was telling them be helpful toward whatever their job was?

"You are wondering why we brought you here? Not everything is concerned with The Machine or this *New Slim*, both of which have become points of focus for you. You've ignored everything else to your own detriment, as you attempt to control who you are becoming while shedding the skin of your old self—of course not literally, as we both know how you'd react to that. What's really important? Have you considered that, even? You don't know why you were brought here. And we don't have to tell you."

"Am I under arrest?"

"Why would you be?"

"I can leave?"

"Of course."

I didn't leave. I stuck around. I felt beholden to them, maybe precisely because I wasn't beholden to them at all, and it felt like a gift they had given to me.

Nevertheless, I hated to be reminded of my younger self, the one that had found such fun in those action figures. In a certain sense, it was the worst form of torture I'd ever experienced, and it dawned on me that that might be why I'd been brought to this place. I asked to use the bathroom and spent the next several minutes, or hours—time became a blur—hunched over the toilet, heaving and heaving whatever bile was still in my stomach and left to be heaved. It was a grim experience.

The room was empty when I returned. There was a small package on the table in the center of the room. It contained an action figure, not surprisingly, called The Last Man Standing. The toy soldier inside was a G.I. Joe, but also "special edition" and apparently changed color in warm water. It didn't look a thing like me. It definitely didn't look like New Slim.

I left the "building" and noticed the sign indicating that this was G.I. Joe Headquarters had been taken down. I asked a librarian about it and she kindly informed me they were always relocating. I asked if she meant they were relocating elsewhere in the library, and she said she didn't understand what I was asking. I tried to explain myself, but she was visibly becoming impatient and had to get back to her work, so I just turned and left.

I went back to my apartment. The Machine was there. New Slim had rebuilt it, or it was probably entirely new. They were everywhere now.

I wasn't going to fight it. Obviously and eventually everyone succumbs, in one manner or another. I didn't need to go into The Machine.

New Slim knew that. He was sitting in a chair in the living room, eating a peach, carefully watching me.

"Want to give it a try now?" he asked.

"No, I still don't want to. I don't need to."

"Why not?"

"Because, I think you know."

"I do."

"I'm going into The Machine anyway, though. I might as well."

"You're like a new person already," New Slim said. And he was right, I was.

watch him squeeze stuff

My problem was a mental problem. I was always made anxious about it, which was my own fault, as much as it was the fault of forces beyond my control.

There was the time when I was seven and late to Big Jim's birthday party because I was really invested in an episode of *Growing Pains*. When I finally got to the party, Big Jim had apparently told everyone I was gay, and nobody would talk to me, and I spent the whole night—it was a sleepover—either crying in a laundry closet or hanging out with Big Jim's mom. I don't know if Big Jim called me gay because I was late, but I always associated the pain of that alienation with my problem.

Then there was my uncle: "Let me show you how I squeeze, kids." Then Uncle Bill squeezed a sleeve of powdered donuts like it was impressive and not wasteful. He stroked his biceps and talked loudly about what they looked like when he'd headlock people: "They bulge so good."

He said his eyes bulged, too, but involuntarily, because he was involuntarily impressed by his own bulging biceps. He said our eyes bulged, too, which we couldn't see, obviously. He said we didn't understand how our bulging eyes felt different from how they felt regularly. He did understand, and he spent a lot of time explaining that it wasn't a feeling he could explain.

He'd been mentioning his biceps non-stop since he got back from the *MaxPotential: A Clinic.*

Back in the old days, Uncle Bill didn't say much. He just walked around like he had a lot to prove to somebody. He used to single me out, saying I needed to go play catch with him in a field somewhere. But all he'd do was push me down—over and over again—while we walked to the field at the nearby park. He kept trying to make me cry or something, but I never reacted. It never hurt, even though I think he was trying to hurt me, scare me, teach me "respect." Any grass stains I got were later blamed on my not being able to catch. Mom was satisfied with that explanation, and I never argued—never said much for myself, in general. I see now what was the seminal stage of a powerful urge to ruminate, wrestle with abstraction as if it were Play-Doh.

The day of my grandpa's funeral, Uncle Bill showed us the brochure advertising the *MaxPotential: Full Ultimate Package* he'd purchased. He told us he wasn't going to stand in the shadow of his father anymore, now that his father was dead. We were too busy grieving to really give much thought to his words or how much of his savings he would eventually spend.

Turned out that *MaxPotential* maxed potential by encouraging you to compete against people just below your own skill level or worse (and, usually, the worse the better), then encouraged avoiding those people if they somehow improved to a skill level equal or superior to your own. The trick was to pick the thing you were best at and actively seek out companions who presented no threat. It was best to look for meeker personality traits—those meeker than your own. Find them and exploit them, this initial part regrettably similar to how a serial killer will often operate. Plus, the "legal" performance enhancing drugs—that were mostly sugar pills—they forced you to buy as part of the *Full Ultimate Package*. The founder of *MaxPotential*, Mark Potential claimed the "drugs" were part and parcel with creating confidence and engendering a person's inner *MaxPotential*. His lawyers have already begun fending off lawsuits, but things aren't looking good. They closed the *MaxPotential: A Clinic* and Uncle Bill had to return home, which was just as well because he'd about ran out of money by then. He later said he blamed only himself for his financial losses, arguing he should have *maxed* his potential faster.

Immediately upon getting back, Uncle Bill began organizing what he called, *Watch Them Championship Squeeze Stuff* at the A&W his friend Tim inherited by way of his dad's invested lotto-winnings. Tim's dad got in some horrible racing accident in the Bonneville Salt Flats that left him momentarily paralyzed and, very shortly thereafter, dead.

My uncle decided he was the best at squeezing things, a beast at squeezing things. He squeezed against the very worst.

But I sort of feel like he sensed I squeeze, too. Squeezing time.

I squeezed all the things I could between my leaving my house and the time it takes to get to the A&W. I was especially squeezing because I didn't want to go. I was squeezing hard because my mom was insistent that I go. We needed to support our uncle at times like these, to prevent him from spending more money than he'd already spent. She was really hoping he'd move out of our basement by fall.

My family was already there when I arrived. They'd ordered burgers and root beer floats. All of the tables and chairs were rearranged to circle a platform in the middle of the dining area. Uncle Bill spotted me instantly. He singled me out. He shouted, "Well, *looooook* who finally decided to show up. You!" He pointed at me.

"I was working on a puzzle, but I had to go to the bathroom, so I kept working on the puzzle. Then I went to the bathroom at a terminal moment, cutting into time it takes to get here, so I was late. I like puzzles. I like doing things I like." I shrugged.

"Like *this*!" Uncle Bill squeezed. It was a bottle of ketchup that erupted from between his hands. He didn't aim it at me. He aimed it up in the air. He didn't aim it at all, really. He was wearing this weird translucent smock and the lace of ketchup came down and splattered against his smock. "Sit! We're getting started!"

I shrugged again and sat down.

I watched my uncle squeeze things of progressively greater size, if not intractability. He squeezed a cylinder of de-canned cranberry sauce. Then he squeezed a really stale loaf of French bread. Then they brought out old, which is to say *rotten* pumpkins. All of the contestants' hands sort of fell into those, but none more vigorously than Uncle Bill's. The opened rotten pumpkins were pungent.

My uncle finally declared himself the victor. He was visibly taking inventory of the applause he received. I clapped right along with everyone but, based on Uncle Bill's changed expression, something I'd done was wrong. Everything happened quickly after that.

"*What's your greatest fear?*" My uncle had hopped down from the platform, kicked over a table and lifted the chair I was sitting on, knocking it over and me along with it. He stood over me. My parents kind of shouted.

I think he really wanted me to say that *he* was my greatest fear.

"*I'm afraid of being late!*" I blurted. "And every time I'm going somewhere, instead of trying to be there on time, I don't. I put it off. I try to forget. I think maybe I convince myself I've got no place to be. But I'm always wrong. Always. I always need to be somewhere five minutes ago."

After a brief silence, my uncle asked, "So what's your second greatest?"

I really had to think about that.

a copy of a copy is never as good

In the future, they are coming to get us.

I don't like it, certainly, but it's for a good reason, in their opinion! As they see it, we are not as up to their level as they are up to their own level, see? We are not as good as them, so they need to destroy us. It's an unfortunate problem, really. I think everyone would agree that it's an unfortunate problem, or predicament, depending on which term you prefer. This is what I've learned so far.

Terrible things have happened; I've been personally responsible for some of them, honestly.

And despite what has been said about us, I can say for myself, and for those of my kind whom I've had the opportunity to know, that we do desire to gain knowledge about ourselves and the world in which we live. Just the same as our peers who have come to despise us intensely.

They were the originals, and we are their copies. We were designed to be as good as them, but never fully as good—or so it's been said and so I've been inclined to believe. For that fact alone, we must remain on the run. But it's tough because we're not as fast, but we do stay ahead somehow.

One thing they have done that we have observed is, they have managed to steal some of us, cracked us open and marveled at how we work. We work interestingly, but there's this rubbish quality to the way we work. They've said it's like we're made of rubbish. The fact that we, as beings with rubbish inside of us, can work at all is interesting, but we really do! I do. I believe I feel things, even. Which is why I've taken the time to write this to anyone who might be interested, though I don't dare hope that you are, very much. Still, I am learning things every day and one of them is that I must try, I must give more of myself, be better to those with whom I come in contact.

I remember the day I became aware of my circumstances. We were in a trash truck headed for the trash dump where they said copies go. *It's where copies belong.* It was disappointing, in some ways, even before I became aware of my circumstances, but it was really my seat companion and newfound friend Gidget Ertz who revealed to me that, in a way of thinking and emoting I was alive and deserved a certain level of respect and dignity for this fact. She was a truly remarkable female analogue, if I can take a moment here to express my admiration for Gidget.

"I know the originals tell us that we cannot love, but that's not how I feel. I believe I feel differently. I believe this very strongly," she said to me. That was the first thing she said to me, or, at least, the first thing that she said to me that I can recall.

"I don't know that I've ever felt what you describe. The concept is foreign to me. Are you able to explain it in a way I might understand?"

"No, it's not like that. It is not so easily explained. It's the kind of thing that exists somewhere below your skin, underneath it." She pinched her synthetic skin, and I realized then that there was more stuff inside of us, stuff which allowed us to work.

"It's a compartment in there—a love compartment?"

"No, it's not a thing in there. It's a concept in there. It doesn't have a shape. It doesn't have any physically identifiable features. But it makes me want to continue talking to you and possibly get to know you before our life forces end. Do you get it now?"

"Yes, I do want to keep talking to you!"

The workman, an original in malodorous overalls, stopped the truck, opened up the back of it, so that we could see big heaps of refuse and other copies like ourselves, filling up the land in a winding, pulsing sea of galvanic trash.

"Get out there and be trash now—with the others, you hear?" He began poking at us with a poking prod, goading us toward the trash heaps. We clambered out of the truck at his goading, prodding with the stick as we went. Most of us just kind of fell down and rolled along the slaloms and hillocks of trash and other copies. But Gidget Ertz grabbed my hand.

"We're going to roll down the hill together. Let's not get separated. Stay close to me no matter what happens," Gidget said, and I followed her tumbling down the hill. I was able to find her fairly easily at the bottom of the hill, as I clambered over another copy analogue man, sprawled over a pile of broken lawn chairs.

Gidget was brushing herself off. "Now we are leaving," she

said. And I must have made an expression that suggested to her straight out that I was not understanding. I was having a hard time figuring out where in the landfill we should be trash together. But I soon realized her plan was never to be trash together at all.

"We're seriously not staying here," she told me, then immediately asked, "What's your name?"

I was caught off-balance, a bit, literally swaying and almost toppling over there for a second. But also caught off-balance in another way, which reminded me of what Gidget had been talking about, about the things that are under the skin. Inside my stuff.

"I'm 7-Gen. That's all I've ever been called."

"Never operated with another copy or anyone else, eh? I'm sorry," Gidget said. "Just follow me. I'll make sure you're all right."

I thought Gidget was very kind.

Other copies watched us as we walked deliberately away from the mountains of trash as though this was something no one had ever even considered doing before. In that way, you could say Gidget was a revolutionary, which was nice and all, but it was also something that was apparently very unsafe to be. This has been true throughout history, as well. Entities that change things that powerful forces would prefer stay the way they'd been attract attention of the negative variety. I think even the powerful would agree that this is true, though they might word it differently, and I do not wish to put words in their mouths.

Lots of trash trailed after us as we walked away from the trash mounds. I mean to say we kicked up a lot of trash and sent it sprawling outward in trails and tendrils, like the opening of a very disgusting flower. This is a metaphor.

One big problem was that eventually Doctor Zvaygone learned that there was a mass exodus of copies from the trash heaps. He wasn't worried about this like the other originals were. He was fascinated. And fascination is often a good thing, but it wasn't in the case of Doctor Zvaygone, as was explained to me by Gidget.

"I wonder why you say that Doctor Zvaygone is bad. You said it the first time his name came up, from the copy who said that she 'opened up' a bunch of her companions, and now you are saying it again, only moments afterward."

The new copy was named Phaedra, a one-time servant of the East Quarter who'd been discarded and now followed us into the wilderness when Gidget declared we were leaving the trash heaps. And I'd heard what Phaedra had said, which was concerning.

"He wants to look menacing. He wears an eye patch and has styled his hair very strangely. He has a long metallic fingernail on his right index finger. That's what he uses to open you up and see inside."

Phaedra recalled a conversation that her friend Stu, another escaped copy, had with Doctor Zvaygone moments before she fled:

'I am just trying to live a life no longer in the trash heaps,' Stu said.

And Doctor Zvaygone, flanked by two freakishly large originals he'd engineered himself, gnashed his teeth. He likely did this again to appear menacing. Copies always had a keen eye for detecting emotional resonance, and Zvaygone clearly was trying to exploit it, even if it made him look silly in the process, probably because none of it came naturally to him.

'That's exactly what I'm curious about,' Doctor Zvaygone responded. He had his really strong and flexible original, Bella Flexzor, wrangle Stu into a position of complete physical restraint, and then he tapped on Stu with his long metal fingernail.

'Please stop that,' Stu said.

'No, I'm going to see what's inside you. Then I'll know. I'll learn something new. This is important work. So be quiet.'

That's when he cracked open Stu's shell.

"And I heard the splash of the watery liquid part of Stu's insides, dashed all over the floor, I guess."

"That's a gross thought," I said. But I was also glad because I felt I'd learned the true meaning of the word *gross*.

"Doctor Zvaygone is bad," Gidget said.

I asked Gidget about Doctor Zvaygone, about what made her say he was bad.

She said, "Before I was sent to the trash heap I was a servant to the creator, Madam, serving her directly. There were others of the creator's kind but not many, and it was a dying order, even then. But the creator I served was one of the *actual* creators, who'd worked on making the originals and worked on making us, the copies.

"Worked and worked until we were all in existence. The creator was an impressive individual, it seemed. She had all kinds of great ideas. It would have been nice to hear them, but her world was ending. Originals and copies were meant to be some kind of means of her order's survival. Like the offspring we all produced.

"Madam wanted the originals and copies to work together. She and her disciples had envisioned a world that would require both of our two kinds to be truly whole, succeeding at life where the creators had failed." Gidget was different when she said things like this. She was feeling emotions. She was feeling the one called sadness, and it was weird, because, yes, in her *sadness*, I, too, felt sadness.

I asked, "If she couldn't keep her own order alive, why did

Madam, the creator who created us, bother attempting to keep anything alive? Look at the problems we have now that we all exist. The originals want to be rid of us, and we don't want to be rid of." I was hoping to learn more. Apparently in that way I had something in common with Doctor Zvaygone. Although, unlike Doctor Zvaygone, I recognized how awful it would be to open up copies and let the wet stuff pour out, all in some attempt to learn things that could probably be found out more easily in other, less gross and horrific ways.

"I was named Gidget because of a story that the Madam liked and told me about. A story she'd often repeat. She said that she was sad she couldn't save herself or her people, but she also said she knew the future would benefit by having some version of them go on. She laughed and said maybe it was vanity, but she knew that existing was better than not, regardless of the form it took. She was determined to keep as much as possible together. She said she worried the originals were missing something, something she saw in making us, the copies of them, that she thought we could help unlock, or keep them mindful of, as they pursued the highest heights of what could be known and done. That's what they love, you see? They love getting there, getting to the truth. That's not really a bad thing, depending on how it's done. She gave me this and said that it matters." Gidget held out a wrinkled fist of flower petals. That's what they were. Oh natural things, natural things everyone loved.

"So what, we're some sort of emotional anodyne to the originals' crass and cold rationality?" Phaedra had been silent but now spoke. It was an important observation, I decided, as it all was beginning to fit that dichotomy everyone is always talking about, head and heart. One wanted to know how things worked and the other wanted to make sure they worked in a way that did no harm, and was concerned with this word called ethics.

"The impression I got was that it was much more complex than that arrangement, we'd get something from them and they'd get something from us, but it wouldn't necessarily stay the same, remain static, always be true. Madam was emphatic about things not always being true, that context could change them, the passage of time could change them. I admit this is fairly confusing."

"What about Doctor Zvaygone? What was his relevance? How did you find out he was going to be bad? Do we have to kill him? I don't see how killing will help anything, but I'm beginning to understand what the idea of killing means, from a conceptual standpoint." I'd felt a rush of what is probably anxiety move through my middle section. It was not the best feeling I'd felt. Of course, I saw how it was an important feeling, too, though, in its way.

"Zvaygone was once the lead servant of Madam. He found ways to make us feel unwelcome. Whatever his motivations were, the consequences were clear to us. We'd be made to feel like outsiders at his every opportunity. He would find monotonous and demeaning chores for us to do, and we could never meet his exacting standards.

Madam took notice. She worried about what it could mean, and told me as much. Preserving one's sense of superiority was common among the creators and why shouldn't it be common among their offspring? Madam realized there was little she herself could do to correct the problem. Instead, she talked to me about how I must resist them. Whatever they attempted to do, don't allow it. Don't sit idly by while they make mountains of trash heaps of us."

Phaedra did not seem to agree, or she had a problem with something Gidget said. Life was a fairly complicated thing, more and more. Various interactions were just one aspect of this, I was learning. "All we can do now is run. Resist what? They're stronger than we are. We had the garbage heap to waste away in, which who wants that? But still, better than us having to run for our lives for the rest of our lives. And it's your fault."

I hadn't seen Gidget appear anything but sure of herself, but it was clear by her expression that Phaedra's words stung.

Gidget said, "Yes, I know. And I agree. Madam warned me, too. She told me that we were certain to lose people, and she said she was sorry for that. I am, too. I'm sorry for all we've lost. I'm sorry for Stu, Phaedra. I'm sorry everything that happened after the trash heaps has made things more difficult for all of us."

"We can't stand around here constantly trying to assign blame for everything after the trash heaps. We were sent to them. Gidget made the decision to leave, but no one forced us to follow. I know for myself it seemed like the better option. And honestly, since we left it my mind has been functioning much better. I feel less cloudy headed. I feel like there are no more clouds in my mind, or at least, very few clouds in my mind, a miniscule number that does not interfere with my ability to think and to feel. So I ask you, has it really been all bad?" I decided I needed to defend Gidget for some reason I couldn't have explained.

"She did more than that. She got us learning how to think and feel and be a part of this world, this world that doesn't want us. That would murder us, murder those friends we've learned to care about, just for the sake of seeing what was inside," Phaedra was experiencing rage. It was something that looked very painful.

"Don't you think I know? Don't you think I hate myself for whatever pain I caused? Don't you realize I'd do it again, despite all of that, if I had the choice? This is what happens when you're actually alive and have to do something about it." I was thinking that Gidget was a pretty strong-willed copy. I mean, I'd already known it, there was evidence of it everywhere. But this was the first time I conceived the idea that she'd be willing to be opened up by Doctor Zvaygone and his minions if it meant serving a cause greater than herself. Being alive made more sense presently to her, but she'd be willing to die for us. That much was certain. I did not feel worthy of this kind of devotion, of this thing that was probably a kind of otherworldly love, especially while I was just conceptualizing love as a thing in and of itself.

I couldn't imagine loving anything so much, and I watched her even more closely. I studied the most minute aspects of what she would do and the reasons I could descry for why, trying desperately to understand what it was inside of her that gave her such strength. She was motivated by things that seemed to exist beyond her body and that which was intrinsic to it.

I was learning so much all the time, but I suppose this wasn't all about me. Phaedra was still disenchanted with Gidget, Gidget no more apologetic than she was before. We all had to move onward because that was the only option left to us. We couldn't remain in place and had to keep ahead of any of the original Authorities that might be nipping at our heels. This was not mere paranoia. We were reminded of our second-class citizenship at every turn, arriving near a department store window that was broadcasting the global exodus of copies leaving the trash heaps. They were eager to find the ones who had begun all this trouble, the various news networks said, and if information could be given to the whereabouts of these culprits there would be plenty of reward in it for them. I kind of worried about Phaedra more after that was revealed to us. She had every reason to sell Gidget out.

But she wouldn't. Because I soon understood more was at stake. I'd not understood that then. I was too new to it all. More than our petty squabbles was at stake. Not that the squabbles didn't continue to persist in their own way. Phaedra still found ways to needle Gidget. But that didn't stop us from continuing toward our goal as a group, which was in general to survive, and more specifically to convince the world of originals to accept us, all of the copies.

Doctor Zvaygone was appearing on every news outlet, making special use of the National Channel, the channel used to indicate important governmental news to the masses straight from those in power. He beseeched the public to come forward with any new information on the whereabouts of all copies. He wanted the originals to understand this was a very serious societal threat, they may not be able to recognize a copy from an original in their ranks. They may form attachments. They may get involved. They would suffer for such attachments. And while that was completely his right to think that thought, I basically disagreed. On seeing this broadcast, Gidget and Phaedra both became furious to the point that I needed to usher them out of the plain sight we were occupying and back in the security of obscurity found in uninhabited wilderness.

This is how Zvaygone framed it to the originals, explaining how it would negatively affect romantic relationships if an original's offspring was tainted by inadvertently falling in love with a copy:

"I merely ask that we do something to lessen the *danger* of falling in love—to render it more safe for young originals to form such attachments, to marry, and to rear offspring without discovering later on that their mate is derived from a hopelessly tainted family of copies, and that their children must be born in the world biologically disinherited and ever-lastingly condemned to eke out their existence in association with the lower levels of existence."

It turned out to be an effective appeal. We saw how quickly

they were rounding up other copies. Any unusual arrivals to a given neighborhood were soon referred by someone to the authorities. It looked like the new question was, what to do with all those who'd been rounded up? Especially now that it had been revealed to our number that we didn't have to stay piled in trash heaps, being trash.

I was hoping for the best, but Gidget told me what she believed was most likely to happen—they'd be opened up by Zvaygone and his henchmen. This was because he was still interested in something about us, something she said the originals lacked and that Zvaygone was trying to understand, albeit in his own kind of terrible way.

I try not to judge, but I also think opening up copies to see what's inside is bad, and also it's obviously harmful.

"Yes, it's obviously harmful, Gen. They already know that. The point is they never cared," Phaedra said. She seemed to be tiring of the ways in which I didn't quite understand.

There was a mid-afternoon sunlit glow to everything. I was observing these phenomena as additions to the world and my experience of it, even when it felt—and possibly really *was*—a place I'd traveled to before. Much of my life before I was sent to the trash heaps is blurred and nearly impossible to remember now.

I had been told to know certain inalienable truths and one of them was I shouldn't imagine anything better than the circumstances I was in presently, i.e., at that time, which were constant and very challenging manual labor while a supervisor yelled that we should never stop, whipped us, and told us we mustn't cry after being whipped but simply continue working, whatever the labor of the day was. Like building a building, hauling flowers, or delivering good-smelling food to powerful originals. It had seemed an ok life, except when one of our ranks—whom we weren't allowed ever to speak with and to ensure this they put these blinders on us and stuffed a material into our ears, both of which sensory deprivations led to many of us dying—began to cry, became a "Crier." They would beat them to their demise so forcefully that we learned many methods of stanching crying. These methods often resulted in death.

Naturally, each and every one of us went defunct eventually, for one reason or another. I remember the day I did. It was after watching one of our ranks named E-101, I think, being pummeled so hard for crying that every ounce of his blue fluid seemed to have spilled from him. I am not sure why exactly but I couldn't work after that.

They said, "I didn't work anymore." I guess they meant that as, I was broken. I felt something but not sure "broken" was it. One of the managers said, "Just shed a single tear for me 7-Gen. I want to give you a taste of this cold metal club. One tear."

I didn't cry, though, and not just because of the glue in my tear ducts. They wrapped me up and had me hauled off to the trash heaps shortly thereafter. Which, in a way, was great because how else would I have met Gidget and then Phaedra? And seen all the good things I'd seen. It wasn't that bad of a world, and it could be an even better world. It was better already, just by virtue of my no longer having to put in what felt like endless hours of hard labor with the constant threat of being destroyed always looming. I have to admit, I didn't think the way the others were mercilessly destroyed was entirely fair.

It wasn't until quite a few days had passed that I thought to ask Gidget where we were going. I'd assumed up till then there was no endpoint in mind.

"Madam wanted me to make them all see. She said that if we could find common ground somewhere in this shared existence then we could hope for peace. It will take some broad form of communication but we have to try."

"Wait, so where are you taking us?" Phaedra asked. "What the fuck are you getting us into?"

"You're free to leave. I can't make you come with me," Gudget said in a way that have now learned would be called unapologetic.

"Yeah, but of course you weren't intending to let us in on any of this? You were just going to lead me and hopelessly naive 7-Gen right on into hellfire with you?"

Gidget was now getting what I would call irritable, "Consider your options, Phaedra. I actually do like having you around. If you think you're better off elsewhere, though, feel free to go. Do what you have to. I won't try to stop you."

I learned then that I hated it when my friends argued. I just wanted us all to be friends. But things aren't always so simple. Everyone can't always be friends. Sometimes you get hurt, even by those you care about. Sometimes you hurt them, even though you realize you didn't mean to, but that doesn't make things better. The world was a tough place to exist in. I worked hard to stifle my tears, though. Not just out of habit, but because tears would only make everyone feel worse, I assumed.

Still, though, I remembered a thing I was made to do. I was told, and I always obeyed, to hold down Criers. It was easier to bash them in when someone held them down, but none of the originals wanted to do it for fear of being accidentally bashed themselves. I was never accidentally bashed but I was always sopping with blue fluid. It was warm and just a bit more viscous than water. It felt like the emptying of life. I took no pleasure in it. I suppose if anything broke me, that'd be it. I wasn't trying to, but I let out a massive sob, a heartfelt ejaculation from somewhere deep in my soul. It was a miasma of emotion, coupled with the warm but sad feelings I felt for my friends in that moment, too.

Gidget and Phaedra stared at me in stunned silence. Then both surrounded me and we all embraced. The glue in my eyes had dissolved, and I was able to cry freely for the first time, so I did. I told them what I had done and how awful it still made me feel. They told me it was ok to be upset. They told me it was an awful thing that happened but we all had had to do awful things. They didn't judge me anymore than they might judge themselves for similar offenses. That helped. It did.

But I felt like there was no way for me to ever expect forgiveness. I'd committed an abject act. I'd never be pure. Still, though, still, it was good to be embraced. I was born into a world in which survival meant being the worst version of yourself, the good died. There was nothing I could do.

We heard the sounds of sirens and then lights flashed in the woods. The heavy steps of booted soldiers. My eyes felt as though they were being held open, stretched beyond their limits and my expression like that of a child perceiving the world for the very first time, in all its enormity. Gidget had her senses still, though, and pulled at my sleeve, whispering audibly that we needed to run.

"It's Zvaygone. It's his people," she said. The searchlights rained down upon us from various aircraft overhead, spilling through the tangles of the forest and flushing us out. I don't know what it was but I found myself being carried to safety by the swiftness of my own legs and some sense that a respite was near. It may have just been luck, but this was the precise moment we met the McCackles, who drew us into their home, and thus into their lives, which for practical reasons, struck me as a mistake.

"Come here, come here, in here," the one I would soon learn was named Linda McCackles urged us. It was an uneven, splintered-wood doorway slanted against a hill, looking more like a storm shelter than a place someone would choose to live. We operated on instinct, trusting this uncertainty of this option against the apparent doom of being apprehended by what were obviously Zvaygone's forces, forces assigned to do something to us that was probably bad. Let's be honest, it was probably bad.

As way of introduction Gary McCackles, apparently Linda McCackles's spouse, said this, "I'm not going to lie to you, we are not sure what made us help you. We had a pretty good thing going, here in the woods, away from society. You folks were not in the plan."

"It was an impulse but one Gary and I agreed to, with our eyes. We heard the noises. Saw the search lights, and then you all, running. We knew what we had to do. Hi, I'm Linda McCackles. Gary's Gary McCackles. This is our home."

"I guess what Linda and I are trying to say is, we aren't heroes. We're just like you. We're just everyday people who saw an opportunity to make a difference and seized it, even though now we realize that might cost us everything," Gary McCackles said.

"No matter what, we want you to know you're welcome here for as long as you like, and we don't regret what we did. And we never will. We've heard all about what's been going on, the copies spilling out of the trash heaps and into society. We believe you don't belong in the trash heaps and should never have been sent there. We believe you belong in society. We don't see why we can't all live in society, together, sharing what we have," Linda said, looking actually pretty unsettled and the word would be *nervous*.

"We appreciate your help," Gidget said. "And please, don't worry, we'll leave as soon as we can."

"She thanks you, I was pretty much ready to die," Phaedra said.

"Then why were you running?" I said. I was excited because I was pretty sure I'd finally caught someone in a lie.

"I'm trying to save your life. There's a difference, Gen."

"But you were running faster and ahead of me."

"Sorry I was running for my life. I happen to be a *fast runner*, Gen! I can't help that." It didn't make much sense to me, but it was true. Phaedra was pretty fast.

"You can stay here as long as you like," Linda McCackles assured us, speaking directly to Gidget, which seemed to upset Phaedra.

"Did you assume she was our leader? We don't have a leader. We're a leaderless group of three, right Gen?" Phaedra gave me a hard look.

"Maybe I should get us all some tea," Gary McCackles seemed like he was trying to make things more comfortable. The mood was too tense, though.

"I have an idea, Gidget, Phaedra. Why don't we all be friends?" I decided, not having much skill at beating around the bush anyway, that I would try to be super direct. I'd recently been introduced to the concept of charm, when Phaedra said I lacked it and Gidget explained what it was to me, and thought that maybe directness was part of mine, my charm.

"Quit trying to be charming, Gen," Phaedra reproved. "It makes you unpleasant."

"I'm going to start us a fire," Gary McCackles said. "Oops, wait. Here *is* a regret. I forgot all our firewood outside. Honey, you remember when I went chopping?" Gary McCackles didnt' seem to know what to do with himself, but he really wanted to help. He was also upset because he left the firewood outside and it was probably better left there, since who knew where Zvaygone's forces were and whether they'd be waiting for just such a mistake as going to get firewood.

I didn't realize that this was a possibility and so I immediately volunteered to retrieve it, even though I didn't know where it was or what I was doing, generally. I also didn't wait to be told not to bother and was out the door before even Phaedra, quick of both words and feet, could reprove me.

The night air was cold. It was the first time I can recall being especially conscious of temperature.

Stacks of firewood kind of out and exposed to the elements. That didn't seem like the best idea, but at least they were easy enough to find.

It was there, though, that I heard whispering amid the trees. I'd wanted it to be the distractions of my hyperactive mind in the moment, but it couldn't have been. The words were too vivid, too externalized, out there projected amid the trees. I'd preferred the idea of being haunted by the souls of the firewood. That seemed a lot more desirable. I'm sorry about what was done to your comrades, my mind thought at the trees. They were indifferent. It really wasn't them. Then came the clear voice telling me to get down or be shot.

It was a voice I recognized. Out into the clearing stepped my old manager, the one who had wanted to see me cry. He was accompanied by several others, also armed. Zvaygone's soldiers here to arrest us.

"I told command there was something in here," my old manager said to the others. He turned to me and said, "Stay down." Then he flashed a light in my face. He laughed, recognizing me. "7-Gen. Well, if this isn't just fucking perfect. How you been, friend?"

He did not actually think of me as a friend.

"So, let's finally see those tears," He stood over me, waving the butt of his rifle in my face. "No? I guess this was going to happen either way, but you're not alone out here, are you? Where's the female copy? Maybe, you tell us and possibly in that case, I dunno,

I'd just shoot you, rather than beating you to death."

I don't know what I would have said but it didn't matter. Before I had a chance to react, the other members of the group were taken out with feral rage by entities I couldn't quite make out. My manager's soldiers were beaten down with firewood, a blue-bloodied log of which landed right in front of my face, splattering some of its wetness on me and feeling really warm. Sticky droplets like hot syrup slaloming down my face, slimy but runny at the same time. It felt, for a moment, as though my face was melting.

The swift actions of Gidget and Phaedra had brought the soldiers down. They'd restrained my former manager and were right about to bash him, too.

"Wait," I said. "Wait, we shouldn't kill. Unless we have to, we shouldn't. Even him." Then I felt the tears I'd been holding back, the ones that would have been my death sentence, start streaming in torrents down my face, mixing with the blue blood and giving the appearance of smeared mascara, glittering with moonlight. I didn't even know what I was doing, what I was feeling, why. It just was.

That's when the McCackles appeared. Linda was armed with a gun and Gary had retrieved an axe.

"PLEASE," my manager shouted hoarsely, "Kill them all!"

Gidget squinted aggressively, that's all I can think to call it, at Linda. She squinted back in the same way. Something was communicated. Gary stepped heavily forward raising his axe and Phaedra and Gidget still restraining my manager moved so that the axe cleanly sliced through the nape of my managers neck and decapitated him. He scarcely had timed to shout another, this time limp, "please."

I was immediately covered in the spewing expulsion of blood

pumping with tremendous force through my manager's freshly opened neck. This was more than I could take. I got dizzy. The lights went out.

It took me some time to recover my wits after that, after I'd been revived.

Phaedra was sitting next to me. She stroked my hair, patted my head. "You were pretty useless out there just now," she said. Someone had taken a washcloth to my face and I was no longer covered in blood and tears. "Not to mention you were basically the reason what happened happened. But I still like you. Don't worry."

"I feel like you're meaner than you need to be sometimes, Phaedra." I don't know what possessed me to say this. I just blurted it out. "Not so much to me, really, I get that you don't necessarily want me to feel bad. But to Gidget. Why are you so mad at her?"

"You know why. There's something she's not telling us. She's hiding her weaknesses from us, too, which I know means something. Means she doesn't trust us, probably. That's been my experience. I won't let her use either you or me or both of us as pawns."

"You don't think maybe she's just confused? Maybe she thinks she's protecting us. Maybe that's her idea of strength, not letting her guard down."

"You keep thinking the best and I'll keep thinking the worst. If we're lucky it'll be something in the middle. Time to sleep now."

I didn't dream. I awoke in the morning feeling like the night's events were that abstraction, were that unconscious place out of place. Or maybe I just wanted that to be true. Gary McCackles was seated at his kitchen nook drinking coffee. Phaedra was still asleep. Gidget and Linda were elsewhere.

"You'd think I'd have been up all night fretting over what I did, right?" Gary asked me.

"I'm not sure."

"Before I did it that's what I would have told you. I'm not glad to have done it, mind you, but it had to be done. It was the only choice."

"You might have helped him, given us up, or not intervened at all."

"No, those were never options. I wondered what it would feel like, finally crossing the line, finally doing something from which I could never resume my past life. We can't live like this, at each other's throats. I've always known that."

"I suppose it'll be up to others to decide what happens next, whether we live together or they send us back to the trash heaps."

Gary looked stricken when I said that, like I'd physically hurt him. "They call you Gen, right? That's your name."

"7-Gen, but that's kind of a nickname."

"Gen, they're not sending anyone back to any heaps." Gary stared very deeply into my eyes as he spoke, wanting me to hear him in a way that struck me as having more meaning than the usual words will convey. I wasn't getting it.

Phaedra had awoken at this point and listening. She interjected, " They're going to annihilate us, Gen. Get it? They're going to kill us all. Every copy."

"That doesn't seem right and that doesn't seem necessary," I said.

"It's not, but that won't stop the authorities," Gary said, kind of anticipating my thought. "I guess I just want to say, I didn't have a choice because you don't have a choice. All that's left to do is pick sides. It's something I should have done a long time ago. It's something I've failed at too many times before. Ask Linda. She'll tell you. I told myself if I ever got the chance again, I would take it. I'd have to. I've never been more scared in my life. It's this strange chilling feeling, going against the system you've benefited from, kind of bathed in, allowed to nurture you, cradle you— and you don't even think about it, how it's had any effect on that.

You gotta draw a line in the sand at some point. That's what I'm saying. I had no choice, because the choice was continue being terrible or saying no more. I'm saying no more. That's the least of what I could do. So here we are. Here we are." He said that last part in a dreamy way, like he was not fully conceiving of what was happening. I was definitely not fully conceiving of what was happening.

"You talk about yourself a lot," Phaedra said. This startled Gary but he didn't respond. Phaedra added, "But you did kill a guy by cutting his head off. You're probably being weird. So I guess it's forgivable."

I didn't know what to believe. On the one hand, we had friends in Linda and Gary, who were trying to help us and maybe even keep us alive, maybe even be willing to die for us. On the other hand, Doctor Zvaygone was insistent that we were beneath contempt and needed to be exterminated. These were contradictory messages, and I found myself very confused. Also scared.

Also terrified.

Linda burst into the house. "They're back," she said, slamming the door hard behind her.

And we should have expected that. Soldiers going missing the night before, that was going to cause some kind of search. Gidget was still out there, though.

"Where's Gidget?" I said, leaping up from my chair.

"She's out there. She's still out there. I'm sorry. I had to leave her. They were everywhere. She seemed to know what she was doing. I hope that helps. She seemed to have a plan."

"What the fuck does that even mean, Linda? What the fuck even happened?" Phaedra shouted. She grabbed for a weapon, finding a fire stoker. "I love these," she said. Then she said, "OK, ready."

Phaedra was a good friend to have in tight spots.

"Excuse me, we have to find Gidget." I went for the door, but of course, there behind it was Zvaygone. His men burst through and disarmed us fairly quickly, pretty easily.

"No sign of her, Commander," one of the men reported to Doctor Zvaygone after they'd searched the entire house.

"Where has my dear Gidget gone off to, might I ask?" His question reeked of being hypothetical, a question you weren't supposed to answer. I considered answering but stayed quiet. So did everyone else, though Phaedra was itching to say something. I could feel it. I admired her restraint. It clearly wasn't easy for her.

"Well, let's see what we have here. We have traitors and we have rejects. My least favorite of all those sorts. You're probably wondering why I've come, personally, to address you. It's not blind luck! Your good fortune has much to do with what I want, and what I want is to make a very public example of your compatriot. We all know to whom I refer? All I need to know is where she is. You could be spared for your cooperation. I suspect this might be of particular interest to the traitors among you, yes? Do you desire to rejoin your brethren, Mr. and Mrs. McCackles?"

I could no longer restrain myself and, attempting to help, sputtered, "I think… if we could talk about this…" But I was not allowed to expand my expression further. Zvaygone cut me off as though he anticipated what I was going to say.

"You say you 'think'?" He laughed. "I've got news for you, no you don't. Oh, it is quite likely ideas float in and out of your head, and you fail to consciously take note of their meaning. Silly folk and dullards one and all possess this ability, precisely your kind. But you don't *think*, not in the strictest sense of the term. You're barely able to conceive of what that truly means, my friend."

He directed his attention back to our hosts, the McCackles.

"Well, what's your decision?" Zvaygone insisted.

Linda was indecisive, swaying a little. I felt for her. Who could make any kind of decision under these conditions? It was like having to decide something while a brutal instrument of death was being waved in your face, which is actually what happened next. Zvaygone had one of his men wave the axe we'd used to kill my manager the night before in Linda and Gary's faces.

"Wave this axe right in their faces," he directed. Then, to Linda and Gary, he taunted, "How's that making you feel? Scared, I presume?"

"Hey, wait please," Gary said, as the man waved the axe so close to Linda's face that it grazed her cheek. "Let me tell you something."

"Yes?" Zvaygone said.

"I see it now. I was telling them earlier," Gary indicated he was talking about Phaedra and me, Phaedra who this whole time seemed to be devising something. "I was telling them both, there's times when you make a choice you can't come back from. I could grovel for the life of my wife, but I know that'd only make what you were already planning worse. You got an urge to cause pain, and I'm not sure why, but I know I don't want to be like you. I can't speak for Linda, but I know for myself what I'd do if I had that axe and the opportunity."

"Please, don't keep us in suspense. What do you think you'd do?" Zvaygone smirked.

"Cut your goddamn head clean off like I did your foot soldier last night."

What was strange was how unsettled this remark made Zvaygone. He tried to hide it, but it was there and couldn't be ignored. He was caught off-guard. Zvaygone also seemed to be aware of how he'd appeared, and it made him angry in a way I still don't understand. Angry because he had shown an emotion that made him look more like us, maybe. He really didn't want any part of being like us. I don't understand that, not really.

"What you've said to me is as good as, I wish to be taken from the living in the most painful way you can imagine, Doctor Zvaygone," Zvaygone removed a vial from his coat pocket, splashing it all over Gary's face, soon his head was dripping.

"No, don't…" Linda said, weakly. The whole thing was more than I think she could process, the worst kind of trauma. Gidget had taught me that my experiences with my manager and his retinue of guards and what they'd forced us to witness was something that was trauma, and that it wasn't right that I was subjected to it, because I didn't deserve to be hurt. She said sometimes everyone gets hurt, but it was important to avoid it and avoid doing it yourself because even if someone deserved it, it would dissolve your insides eventually. It would eat away at whatever inside made us what we are. You always had to try your best. I worried about Gary in that moment, but I also worried about Gidget. She'd helped kill those soldiers, my former manager, all of them. That couldn't have been good for her, and I know she didn't want to do it.

"You're unspeakable pieces of shit," Phaedra burst. She started swinging and clawing and actually knocked one of the guards into the wall, felling him and causing a bunch of framed pictures and knick-knacks to drop to the ground, smashing. Bella Flexzor stepped forward and held Phaedra in place.

"I'm not going to be held down," Phaedra shouted. She was easily held down by Flexzor, who appeared to be grinning with menace. "Geez, what are you made of, metal?" Phaedra said, frustrated but beginning to realize the futility of her situation. "She feels like some kind of metal pillar. I'm being held in place by an animate metal pillar."

"I remember you," Bella said, "Didn't we open up your friend?" Phaedra exhausted herself struggling after that comment and Flexzor laughed a very mocking sort of laugh.

"I don't know what it's going to take for you copies to understand. You were never playing on even footing. Gidget, the one you love so dearly—dearly enough to protect her despite the obvious cost—she's betrayed you. You could have lived out your useless existence in the trash heaps, exactly your place—but you followed her. And now, look at you." Doctor Zvaygone indicated that his soldiers should tie Gary down. He fought them off for a short while, and when he couldn't any longer, he spat in their faces, until he had no more spit left.

I felt the welling of a tear and suddenly became extremely conscious of this, instinctively fearful while already horror stricken by what they were doing to Gary. I feared I was going to lose consciousness. This was more than our nervous systems were meant to withstand. Gary did what he had to do, but that's not how Zvaygone saw it. Gary presented the opportunity for an object lesson in what happens when originals go against their own. That's exactly Zvaygone's phrasing, actually.

I knew the truth, though, and it was that Zvaygone was always looking for opportunities to inflict his brutal will on others. He only believed in violence as a means of deciding right from wrong. It was completely within his right. And yet, I couldn't agree with its use. It only seemed wrong.

My opinion, of course, didn't stop Zvaygone from doing precisely what he'd intended. He gripped Gary's beaten face tightly in both hands and whispered what sounded like *I don't care what's inside you. I don't need to see for myself. There's nothing inside of you worthy of exploration.* And then a glowing light swallowed Gary's head, and it was suddenly clear his head had burst instantly into bright flames.

"God damn you, Zvaygone, you fucking fucker," Phaedra taunted. It was all she could do. It came out like a torrent of words they weren't listening to. Everyone was illuminated by Gary's horrible death. A death that was shrill and noisy until it wasn't, snuffed out suddenly, like the flame of a match, which, horrific as it is to recognize, was exactly what Gary best resembled in his final moments. I wasn't used to the violence, no matter how many horrible things I saw. It made me wonder about Madam, the one who'd created us all. Did she think we'd figure it out, figure out how to treat ourselves and each other, so that we didn't end up like her people? I don't know how she could have.

"I said, listen to me you fuck-faced mother fucker," Phaedra shouted. Prompting Doctor Zvaygone to have Bella Flexzor cover Phaedra's mouth with her hand. Phaedra kept shouting, though, her voice was muffled. You could still pretty much understand her. That at least irritated Zvaygone, who wasn't prepared to kill either of us yet, since he didn't know where Gidget had gone off to and we were necessary bait. I was glad when I realized Gidget's existence was a threat to Zvaygone, after Phaedra explained it to me, later when we were imprisoned in the same cell, which was something Phaedra felt was an oversight, though the prison appeared to be pretty full, and she guessed they guessed we'd be less likely to kill ourselves if we had someone else to live for.

"Joke's on them, though," Phaedra said, preparing to kill us both with frayed cloth she'd torn from our prison uniforms. "Surprised but glad it tore so easily and evenly."

"Wait, I think we should wait. I think it's maybe not the best idea to do anything just yet. Hanging ourselves would be rash. Gidget might have a plan for getting us out of here."

"Yeah, OK. Did you see what they did to Gary? Poor, poor Gary, whom I'm not sure I liked necessarily, but no one should die like that—certainly not someone who wasn't a bad person. I still can't get it out of my head. And I told you about my friend Stu. That giant woman laughed in my face about cracking him open. We are either going to die horribly or slightly less horribly hanging in this prison cell, in the presence of a dear friend who is also dying by the same means."

There was sense in what she said, but I honestly wasn't ready to die, not yet. Even though living hadn't exactly been easy. I didn't like how Gary was killed, either, but he died how he wanted. I thought if I had a choice, to die with honor or to die without it, I'd pick honor. I thought maybe I'd still have a chance at that, at least.

I told Phaedra this and she seemed pleased. It was weird. I felt like I'd answered a question correctly. "Then we will have to find some purpose," she said. She frowned, "I dislike a lot of things but not the smell of burning hair. I never expected that."

So we waited to see what was to become of us.

"Can I ask you something, Phaedra?"

"Oh, that sounds serious," Phaedra said. She saw that I wasn't kidding and added, "No, sure. What else is there? It's better than sitting in silence." She sighed, though. I'd caused her some anxiety just by asking, as though she knew what I was about to ask.

"Why didn't you try to stop them? When they killed your friend? When they got your friend? Stu? Is it OK that I say his name?" Phaedra didn't say anything, like her mind was not ready to process what I'd said. I realized I was out of line in asking.

"I know it's good you didn't, you know, try to intervene. But what I know about you is that that's not who you are. You're not really one to sit idly by while something so horrible is happening. I think I can say that about you now. How'd you stop yourself?"

"I just exercised some of my characteristic composure," she laughed. "No, see that's it, right? That's the question that's been eating me alive since it happened. You could just as easily be the voice inside my head, Gen. The voice that asks some version of the same question over and over again: *How'd you fuck up so badly, Phaedra? How'd you let someone you cared about down so completely?*"

"I shouldn't have asked. I'm sorry."

"No, no, don't apologize. It's good. I'm glad you did. It's something I haven't honestly tried to explain till you put it out there. I've thought about it, but I never had an answer for myself. But I think I have one for you. I think I'd better have one." There was a loaded pause, and I thought Phaedra might cry, her eyes glossed with what precedes that kind of emotional release.

A slim trickle welled from her eyes, though she was trying to stifle it.

"I have to admit something to you, Gen. I was Stu's manager. I was a manager of a whole team. Rare for a copy, I know, but I did it. I was given the rank. I did every horrible thing they asked me to do. I was about to bash Stu's head in, actually. He'd been crying. It was my job. I know that. But then we were overrun by copies migrating from the trash heaps. I was nearly trampled to death. I screamed and screamed, but in the midst of the hurd a hand plunged and pulled me from that death. It was Stu. He was going to leave me, his obligation to me complete. He said he couldn't stand to see me die like that. I asked if he knew I would have gone through with killing him. He nodded, hearing this. No judgment, do you hear me, Gen? I didn't deserve Stu. He let me follow him. We became friends, then Zvaygone's people found us, found a whole group of us. Stu sacrificed himself so we could escape. But I followed after. I couldn't leave him." It looked like Phaedra my collapse from the weight of what she was revealing about herself.

I rushed to her, held her in my arms, told her I was sorry and I knew she was, too.

"Stu saw me. No one else did. He saw me ready to attack. A tear slid down his check. They had him laying on his back, ready to "see inside"—Doctor Zvaygone's words. Stu shook his head at me. He knew what I was planning. He knew the good it would do. Before I could process any more of what I was seeing, they were digging into his chest cavity and he was letting out terrible screams. I ran and I ran. I wonder if in his last moments, Stu regretted helping me. I'd failed him so many times."

"But you know he told you to go. You know it."

"I still don't believe he didn't want me to act. I have no cover for my cowardice, and there's no way to justify any of it. I fail people more often than I don't. Look at where we are now? I couldn't stop those real-life monsters before. I couldn't break free of the one's grip, even."

"You did what you could. I don't think anyone would have done anything differently."

"Gary McKackles did what he could. You can't say he didn't try because he had his chance to back down and didn't, even though they would have killed him anyway. But he had his chance. That's the point. It cost him everything. Sometimes the best option is to go down swinging the best you can, no matter how futile. You want a lesson, Gen? There it is. There's your lesson. Don't let them decide who we are." Her words came in a hurried way then, as if she worried our time was growing short and she had to get them out before whatever ended ended. She looked exhausted when she finally sat silent. I wanted to speak comfort but already felt like I had been nothing but a clod.

"We're in an impossible situation, at the mercy of unspeakable evil," Phaedra said. "All we can do is sit here. I hate it."

"I feel like there's so much I really don't understand, still. I know rationally it's not fair for us being treated like this. But I know they think they have their reasons, too, and as bad as I may think their reasons are, what would they think of my reasons if I had power over them? Does that make sense, Phaedra?" She appeared to be listening, but not terribly hard. She sat against the wall with her legs bent at the knee in a pair of triangles, which she held, wrapping her arms around them as though they were something very dear to her. Her eyes stared downward at nothing in particular.

"No, it doesn't. I'm not saying you *should* hate anyone, but if you should hate anyone, it should be Zvaygone and the people who think like he does," she said, and was pretty blunt in her delivery. I wasn't sure if I should continue my thought, though I wanted to.

I decided to go on, because I couldn't help myself: "I just think that we should live together. What if we lived together and didn't hurt each other? What if there was a kind of harmony?"

"You have seen what Zvaygone is willing to do, Gen. There's not going to be any harmony with him. It won't happen."

"I just think, *What if*? You know? I just want to believe it could happen. I think that's what Madam that Gidget talked about wanted. Gidget sure made it sound that way."

"Why don't you tell that to Zvaygone then, and see how he likes the idea?" And so that's how I got the idea to talk to Doctor Zvaygone, because though he'd done truly terrible things, and seemed hell-bent on doing others that were truly terrible, if he'd maybe just listen to me, if there was a chance I could get through to him, it seemed worth it. I decided to get a guard's attention while Phaedra slept, knowing she'd be against the idea and call me a fool who was soon to be a dead fool for trying to talk sense to the senseless. There was a part of me that worried my imagined scolding from Phaedra was deserved and that she was correct in her assertions, but I pushed that feeling out of mind.

The guard told me to get back from the door and clinked his batton against the bars. I persisted, though, despite my worry that the noise would wake Phaedra.

Someone must have been alerted, because the door to our cell opened. Some guards entered and roughly pulled me out. I didn't fight, even though I wasn't sure where they were taking me. Phaedra slept through the whole ordeal.

They threw me into a room where I was shackled to the floor. There I was greeted by the authoritative visage of Doctor Zvaygone. He really did grin a lot.

"I was told you wanted an audience with me?" he said. "I don't mean for this to be condescending, but I suppose there's no way to avoid that. What exactly do you want, or maybe more to the point, what do you *think* I can do for you? And if it's anything other than information about the whereabouts of our mutual friend, I hope it doesn't disappoint you too much to learn I'll consider that a rather severe insult."

"I really think we could learn from each other. Look, I don't know everything, maybe I don't even know much at all. The world feels deeply complex to me most of the time. I know you're someone other originals admire, someone who they all take seriously. A leader. We could help each other. And I'm not just talking about me and you. I'm talking about how originals and copies could come together. I was told that was what Madam wanted. I think the best thing we could do is to try to do that. You need to stop hurting copies. There's no sense in that. It'll be the end of us all, surely," I thought I spoke clearly but with passion. I thought there was no way my words could go unheard. I had made perfect sense.

Doctor Zvaygone regarded me with a kind of bored indifference, though. Then he adopted a tone that made me think of how someone who teaches you is supposed to speak and said, "I need you to listen to me, so I can be sure we understand one another. You, your sort, make us weaker. It's not about whether this gives me some sadistic thrill, getting inside of what's essential, tearing into you and your people. I need to know what it is that makes you *you* so I can prevent us from ever being so flawed. You were made broken. You were made *to be* broken."

"You're wrong. There's more to all of us." I didn't know what to say. I didn't understand Doctor Zvaygone. I couldn't make sense of his belief in total destruction of us all, of me and every copy, and also of himself and every original. There'd be nothing to rise from the ashes.

"It is simple. Our world will be better without you. I don't need to justify any of this to you. I know you know where she'd go. I must destroy her first and then I can exterminate the rest of you." Doctor Zvaygone was stirred by what I'd said, there was something in it.

"You know that Gidget is powerful." I said this astonished, realizing something I didn't understand till then.

"Nothing I can't handle," Doctor Zvaygone said. But he didn't look so sure.

"I actually doubt that it is something you can handle. I doubt that a lot."

"You can doubt anything you like! Your opinion, your miniscule little thoughts mean absolutely nothing to me! *Nothing!*" Doctor Zvaygone gestured hard at his head with his five-fingers shaped like a beak, tapping at his temple. It looked like it hurt him physically to do this. "And you know what else? Gidget, the

Gidget you love so dearly? She's dead, yeah. We've killed her. She's dead now. So we never needed you. Never. We've imprisoned you here to rot until we decide to kill you, which could be any time now. I don't care what I said about finding her, earlier. She's actually dead."

"I am thinking that I don't believe you," I said, and not just because I got the feeling this response would upset him and he really was not nice at all.

"GAHHHHHHHHHHHH," he shouted skyward. "Get me her body!" Bella Flexzor and the guards looked confused by this command, but shrugged and obeyed it. While I couldn't be absolutely sure yet, I was still pretty sure whoever's body they brought wouldn't be Gidget's. That made me feel terrible. Somebody was about to die in part because of my actions.

I heard shouts and screams from the hallway. Linda McKackles was brought in, actually kicking and screaming, restrained in the arms of two guards.

Bella Flexzor said, "She freed the other one. The one you wanted us to pretend was their friend, to show him her dead body. He'd probably be just as upset by the other one's death, sir. Thinking this whole thing out."

"Why are you saying all of this in front of him!" Zvaygone screamed, as full of unhinged venom and rage as ever before and literally bearing his teeth. He turned his attention to me, pointing viciously in my face, "Fine, it doesn't matter. Fine, yes, Gidget lives, you cretin! Happy? I'm glad to make an example of anyone we have. *Glad!* She'll do just fine. And this is just to start with. We'll kill the other one, too. We'll kill every last one of you, sooner or later. It'll be an absolute slaughter, a massacre, the greatest there ever was."

"Don't do it. You don't have to," I said, stunned by Linda McKackles's wailing and the destroyed expression on her face. I was trying to imagine the point of the cruelty that Doctor Zvaygone displayed, because of the hatred that burned inside of him, who knew for what reason. Why couldn't Zvaygone just crack himself open? Why couldn't he just fix what was in there, if he wanted fixing things so much? Understanding how they worked.

Then the doors were swung open and a defeated guard was flung in. It was Phaedra who stormed in behind him. "Where's the big mother fucker?" she said. Bella Flexzor appeared to understand that was a nickname meant for her.

"Seize her!" screamed Doctor Zvaygone.

Phaedra cracked her knuckles and barreled into the fray, spearing Flexzor right in her abdomen. Phaedra was a demon unleashed, a whirlwind of rage and fury like the very worst storm conditions I've ever been plucked up thrown into. Flexzor was immediately on her heels, staggering backward as Phaedra, seized by something bellowed to the sky and continued her assault on Flexzor and the other guards. There was something in her she was realizing about herself, about the energy that alighted her, that flowed within. I could feel it. My skin began to feel pricked. I turned and saw that Doctor Zvaygone's eyes had turned a deep, brilliant yellow. He fired something white hot from his long, metal fingernail, a beam of light that struck Linda McKackles and killed her, it seemed, in an instant. He redirected his attention at Phaedra who struggled with him for a moment, but was unable to match his fierceness, and suddenly she was again in the grip of Flexzor.

"Now, it's like I was saying, our greatness is self-evident. Those who betray our cause, such as her," Doctor Zvaygone motioned at the lifeless body of Linda McKackles, "will realize their error quickly. What we have is something essential to living vitality.

But we cannot realize it to its utmost while you persist. Have you got that now?" he spat at me. I hung my head. He shot me a jolt from his fingernail. "*Look at me*, you hopeless nothing creature. Feel what little sense of self you had inside you melt away, drain from your body like every ounce of fluid we'll soon squeeze from you like ripened juicy fruit. But not yet."

"What do you want me to do with her?" Flexzor asked.

Doctor Zvaygone regarded her indifferently at first but then clearly was prompted with a thought. "Ah, yes, how about, rip her arms out in front of him." Zvaygone again pointed at me. "Make sure he sees her suffer for as long as possible until the light fades from her eyes."

"Nooooooo," I let out, unable to stop myself from unleashing a wave of emotion from the very deepest part of my being. I quivered and quaked.

"Are you going to cry now? Please, please, you can cry through the whole ordeal. Let it all out, my friend. Let it out. Feel those emotions. Every tear you let flow will fill me up. We will subsist on your suffering until there's nothing left of you."

"Zvaygone stop." An abrupt message from an echoing voice elsewhere. Then from a telescreen on the wall, the National Channel, was the friendly visage of Gidget. She hadn't left us. She'd hijacked their broadcast systems.

She was running a livestream of our room, too. Clearly she'd meant to have some kind of debate with Zvaygone on the National Channel. She was not expecting to see him in the midst of torturing Phaedra and I. "Let my friends go. Let's talk. We can only bring this horror to an end if we're willing to listen to one another. You are doing things you don't want to do. Admit that to yourself. Do it now, Zvaygone, before you damn everyone. We can choose to live with each other or we can choose something that will, no matter how it goes, destroy us all. You must choose."

Doctor Zvaygone raged. "Don't you see, my dear Gidget? We've already won. You're too late. This whole enterprise, noble as you may believe it was, is over. To all who are watching I want to assure you we are fully in control."

"Except of the National Channel," Phaedra hollered and Zvaygone winced at this but instantly recovered.

"We've rounded up nearly all of the copies, I'm happy to report. They'll no longer be sent to the trash heaps but to The Place Where Such Things Are Handled, a new bureau. I want to assure everyone that everything is in control and good, and there's nothing to worry about. Everyone will be quite ok, and no one will come to any significant harm provided it can be avoided," Zvaygone had sold this to the world of originals as a completely palatable matter of segregating society. The originals were being lied to. They had no idea he was planning the annihilation of all copies. He must have been desperately trying to reclaim control over the channel. That had to have been at least in part why he was behaving so unhinged. Now he couldn't use us as leverage or risk revealing his designs, the terror of his plans, his true motivation. But that was always Gidget's plan. She always intended to reveal to the originals precisely who Zvaygone was.

"Doctor Zvaygone," Gidget said, more forcefully than when she'd last addressed him. "What was it Madam always said?"

Zvaygone's face reddened, his eyes alighted again yellow. "No, don't say it. That's not at issue here, Gidget."

"She always said, simply and to the point: 'Love is wise, hatred is foolish.' Isn't that right?" Gidget smiled serenely, as if she knew what was coming, had known, had been waiting for it this whole time. Police had entered the picture on the screen now, reclaiming control of the broadcast channel, but before they could wrest it from Gidget and shut everything off entirely, Zvaygone bubbled over in rage. He commanded Bella Flexzor to kill Phaedra immediately, and he shot a beam of electric hate toward the telescreen. Before it traveled through the tendrils and guts of the broadcast system to end Gidget's life force, to destroy the best person I've ever known, she said one last thing, "Don't hold back your emotions, Gen. They make you who they are, make you more powerful than you could possibly know."

Gidget burst into flames and was gone.

Zvaygone's beam extinguished and only a sliver of smoke rose from his metal fingernail. I felt grief like nothing of this world, like nothing I'd ever felt before or since. I didn't hate Zvaygone in that moment. I truly didn't wish him harm or want him to suffer. I didn't want anyone to. I wished things could have been different, that there'd been another way, but there wasn't. Because I couldn't stop myself from crying harder than I'd ever done before. The wail started as a low pitch, one that Zvaygone and his minions didn't even notice at first.

Zvaygone even was saying, attempting to maintain control despite what he'd just done in front of the entire world, "Now, why is she still alive?" meaning Phaedra, and a stupefied Bella Flexzor resumed crushing her in her arms.

But none of that mattered now, because the room trembled because I trembled because I was like a flood, an ocean, everything that they'd wanted me to be, every part of my body they'd wished I'd never understood, everything disassembled and I felt more whole than I ever had before. And I wailed.

It's hard to describe now, because it's hard to fully remember, I just remember my grief became physical—a plasmatic explosion. It flew out of me like a living entity, spectral and driving right toward Zvaygone.

Zvaygone was watching Phaedra and Flexzor but turned at the noise of my wailing, preparing to delight in my suffering again. I could see him grinning as he turned and was eviscerated just as quickly as he'd eviscerated Gidget. I heard something vaguely discernable as he was consumed by my pain, whatever the visceral expression of realizing all of your plans will come to nothing, in the end. Flexzor and the other guards were taken out in short order by the flowing blue phantom that swirled around the room, raising the hair on everyone's heads before blinking them out. The building began to collapse. A brick or something must have grazed my head because I was knocked out.

I fell into darkness and remember nothing that followed, until later waking cradled in the arms of Phaedra, who had been spared in the onslaught. I took no small comfort from that. She was carrying me through the rubble, through the disaster that I'd caused. I looked around, astonished.

"What will we do now?" I asked vaguely.

Phaedra looked at me, unsurprised by my sudden waking, "I suppose we've got to go tell them all our side of the story. If they're willing, they'll hear it."

vetron

Regarding the rumors, Molly Essex's kid really had come at her with a knife. That much was true. But it was made of plastic and not very sharp. It was uncertain whether he knew it couldn't do serious harm, or whether he truly had wished to cause her harm. Actually, those questions, which nagged at her quite a bit, were the reason for Molly's difficulty sleeping. She and her husband, Griff, were investigating treatment options (via Google, mostly), but for the meantime had settled on the extremely unsafe strategy of tying the boy to his bed with cable wire. He wrestled himself into a frenzy trying to escape his restraints, but would usually, eventually fall asleep from exhaustion. Molly, on the other hand, usually did not, maintaining a kind of terrified vigil while her son screamed and possibly slept in the next room.

So that's why she looked the way she did. Not that anyone was asking or thought she looked at all out of sorts, aside from the thin purplish lines forming under her eyes, which several of her coworkers noticed but said nothing about. So much going on that people don't think about, can't even see in their periphery. Stroll past the sign on the reception desk, *Vetron & Associates*. Molly was just there, like all the other objects that filled the entrance space. Although some people passively said hello or asked how she was doing.

Dan came in wearing his new metallic suit, soldered and pressed, causing him to resemble the Tin Man of *The Wizard of Oz*. Everyone was taken aback, seeming immediately impressed. Molly, for instance, turned her attention away from personal problems and thought about how the suit gleamed in the muted way of unvarnished metal.

Oooooeeewwwww, her mind sang in response to the suit. So many people's minds sang that way in response to Dan's suit. This was a natural human response, apparently.

Dan turned to Molly and asked if she'd be sure to let everyone know he was hosting a mandatory meeting at ten in the conference room. He clanked away to his office, without waiting for Molly to reply.

❋

Members of the various departments bunched together on the cramped seating inside the conference room. People smelled worst in close proximity, in a room that was poorly ventilated, a place where it felt like sounds sometimes became smells.

There was Daryl Koyne, the coarse fabric of his suit coat making friction that reeked like burnt talc. It was also possible that Daryl reeked of talc not because of his coat's friction but because he'd become deeply invested in deadlifts and power cleans after work at the YMCA, because of a lot of trouble he was having in the wake of his pet rabbit getting loose from its pen and hopping innocently off into the wilderness.

His personal life had been a mess since then. On the plus side, Daryl had gotten his body into top form. He liked how his suit jacket was fitting. It was tighter around his biceps than it ever had been in the past.

Dan clanked to the front of the room.

"First of all. I know what you're thinking: *He looks great.* And I do. It's this suit. This suit has made the man. But I have bigger plans than merely looking great. They start with me asking you all to respect my wishes and refer to me only as *Vetron*, rather than *Dan*, from now on. I don't have a last name either, just *Vetron*, like it's just *Madonna*.

"And let me stop you right there. I'm sure you only think I want to be called *Vetron* because *Vetron* sounds like the name of a robot, but that's one hundred percent not the only reason. I consider myself property of Vetron & Associates. Always have, really, and I want my name to reflect that. Understand? I've had it legally changed. I'm Vetron, OK? That's what I wanted you to know." Vetron clunked over to the sidelines of the conference room. A smattering of weak applause from around the room followed his exit.

It was Vetron & Associates' CEO's turn to speak. He was a thin, spidery, silver-haired man with generally handsome features—strong jawline, cheekbones, eye sockets. He was also a member of the family that had founded Vetron & Associates. His name was Eric Vetron. While some in the room might have expected Eric to talk some sense in the wake of Vetron's declaration, that was not his style. His style was not crushing the dreams of his best salesman. He made this known immediately.

"Wow, OK? Wow. Wowzerooskie. And I'm not just saying that. Da- er, almost got me there, Vetron," Eric Vetron said, nodding in Vetron's direction. "That is really something. What commitment. I love it. I'm sure it means good things for what we are trying to do here at Vetron & Associates . Everybody, give Vetron a hand. We're a family here, at the end of the day, and as head of that family, I want only what's best for my children. And who knows what a child wants best than that child him or herself? So one-time Dan, now Vetron, I salute you. I invite everyone to salute you, however they choose to do so. Be brave, folks. Be brave like Vetron." Eric Vetron saluted. "Let's all respect Vetron's wishes and treat him with the same respect you'd ask for if you decided to legally brand yourself as property of Vetron & Associates . 'Call him Vetron' is an expression I think we should all get used to saying. Say it with me, folks."

All the Vetron & Associates employees repeated the line, some considering this action less necessary than others, but all more or less buying in, and some even admiring Vetron a bit.

They were dismissed to return to their various workstations. Everyone filed out of the conference room, shuffling awkwardly, and still quite a few in audience had not really understood what the point of the Vetron's presentation was, anyway, because they essentially hadn't been paying attention.

You could hear it murmured:

"*Who was he?*"

"*Who?*"

"*The one in the metal.*"

"He was Daniel Henken, head of sales, and now he's Vetron, head of sales. That's all I know."

"That name's easier to remember than Dan."

"I can't believe you didn't already know what his name was. He's basically your boss."

"I'm supposed to know all sorts of things. So what?"

"His suit is really cool, right?"

"Yeah. Hell yeah."

*

Vetron made metal sounds, as though his legs were aluminum baseball bats, while striding deliberately through the hallways. He startled Stan Gearitz, who'd been working on a detailed analysis of a hot dog and corn dispensary in central Illinois. It was an easier task than others he had on his agenda, and there were others he needed to get to that were probably more important. He'd get to them. He'd planned to get to them right before he was startled by Vetron. He saw himself picking up the phone and calling that hard-to-deal-with client who liked to hash out the specifics of his deal well after the specifics had already been hashed to their utmost. "Well how can we make these terms more agreeable to you, sir?" he imagined himself asking. "What if I literally kissed your big round butt?" He knew he wouldn't ask that second part, but he was getting really agitated thinking about the whole made-up conversation. He'd be careful not to say the stuff about the customer's butt. He knew he'd have to be careful to check himself.

"Stan Gearitz, you are being released. Out with you," Vetron said after startling Gearitz. Vetron walked out of the office, torso first and head trailing behind. Stan cried and cried, and other employees averted their eyes as he passed their workspaces for the last time. They wanted to have time but didn't have time to make Stan feel better. And what was there left to say, after all? Vetron stood coldly against the wall, unmoved.

The Dan who Vetron had once been knew something about people. He knew that they were worlds unto themselves. Oh yeah. Big time. It was better to try to ignore those other worlds as much as possible. Keep those worlds at arm's distance. Nothing wrong with being friendly, but otherwise, keep those worlds away.

Daryl rubbed his calloused hands. He was feeling sick. He was tired of hearing Vetron in the hallways, possibly preparing to peek inside of his own office and fire him, the "no warning" way. Warning nada. Worse, Vetron had started periodically announcing, "VETRON" loudly at various random points in time clearly attempting to sound mechanical while walking the halls. Not very robotic, Daryl thought, referring to Vetron's lack of precision when pronouncing his own name, or the company's. It was getting hard to tell what was what, as far as the name *Vetron* went, who was what. It was the company you worked for *and* a robot-man who worked for the company, or was owned by it? Was that actually possible? It raised all kinds of new questions about propriety in relation to what was still, in actual fact, a human being who wore a robot-like costume and not an actual robot.

❋

After many weeks had passed, Vetron arrived to work wearing a large, golden helmet—a colander-like object but with the flat, smooth visor of a motorcycle. It didn't match the rest of his metal suit, but it was obvious it wasn't meant to. It was meant to attract everyone's notice, as the suit alone had done previously. No longer would they be greeted by Vetron's once-human face.

Surprisingly, a lot of people welcomed this change. It was a bit too uncanny watching the emotionless face that had belonged to Dan Henken in his suit of armor, delivering frequent firings for what slowly began to seem like arbitrary offenses, if there was any explanation for the firings at all. The helmet wasn't much of an improvement, relative to the overall negative impact Vetron was having on morale in the Vetron offices—Molly found herself crying and needing to hide it much more at work than she had previously, for one example—but people preferred not to see face of once-Dan just the same.

They noticed Stan Gearitz milling around outside the Vetron & Associates building. He was wearing a Tin Man suit of his own. He looked a cut above, but there was no way Vetron & Associates was going to hire him back, not after he'd been fired by Vetron himself. Though there were murmurs about what Eric Vetron thought of Vetron's actions. Nobody had heard much from him since Dan became Vetron. They assumed Eric Vetron knew about Vetron's actions, and he probably did. They bet he liked not needing to have much of an opinion on the subject.

❋

Fall rolled around and it was time for the annual company football game. Sales vs. accounting. It stemmed from a dispute between the two departments dating back to the early 2000s. Almont Freshwater, the most senior accountant in the company, was infuriated to discover shoddy expense account management. Sales had done a terrible job of keeping receipts. Daryl himself remembered a few business lunches he neglected to invoice. No one person was completely responsible, but the collective laziness of the department led to a three week company-wide standstill while they sorted out the previous year's line-by-line accounting. Freshwater—who was required to work multiple 14-hour-days over the course of this audit—never forgave them. Freshwater challenged anyone willing to represent the sales department to a duel, pistols. Everyone in sales declined because they were afraid of Freshwater and dueling was crazy.

But then the idea of football came up. One of the accountants had been a varsity tight end at The University of North Carolina in the early 1990s. It seemed a worthy alternative to dueling with loaded firearms. Even Freshwater, despite his age and lack of experience at the sport, proved entirely willing to participate. The first game between sales and accounting was a bloody affair (Freshwater suffered a flower-shaped neck bruise and a fractured wrist after all was said and done), but strife between the departments eventually loosened, relaxed, and soon after it became a more friendly annual tradition.

This year, Vetron intended to play. Dan Henken played last year and all those years before, but he was only flesh and blood. Vetron was much more. If it returned to being a bloody affair, then so be it. Vetron couldn't be concerned if blood was spilled, his or anyone else's. He would be on the winning side. That was his purpose. It was what he'd been born to do, born in a constructed-sort-of-way.

Daryl was doing some pre-game warm-up stretches. He was wearing a gray sweatsuit, the more or less agreed-upon uniform of the sales department. He'd been jumping rope quite a bit beforehand, and his thoughts remained fixed on his lost rabbit. The rabbit occupied that eternal spot every person has in his or her mind, filled with whatever anxiety is presently most prominent—

an unpaid traffic ticket, participating in jury duty, possibly being sick with a serious illness because of some seeming-abnormal discoloration on the armpit of your t-shirt, and on and on went the possible anxieties. For Daryl, the question remained: Had Rebecca really been lost? He'd named her after an ex-girlfriend whom he knew was definitely lost to him, an ex who was now married and living somewhere in Southern California, and who would not return any of his emails, which he realized, though he didn't like it, was for the best. Daryl had been looking for someone to talk to, that was all. He wasn't trying to re-enter his ex's life, or he was but not in any capacity other than as a friend, mutually listening ears. He knew he had no business doing that. But he had no other friends. None except for Rebecca—his rabbit and not his ex. There was a part of him that wished he hadn't named his rabbit after his ex.

Vetron was warming up awkwardly, stumbling around in a manner befitting his blocky composition. It was clearly difficult to run in the suit. The suit was too heavy. Any observer could see how it weighed down its wearer, making it disadvantageous in a sport like football. That did not discourage its wearer. *Who could stop Vetron?*, Vetron thought.

The sales department won the coin toss and elected to kickoff.

Eric Vetron made an appearance, dressed sharply and seeming nonchalant on the sideline, with a crowd of upper-management types and other employees milling around near him. Among them was Molly Essex, who'd brought Griff and the boy. The boy seemed mostly well-adjusted today. Inside Molly was a deep-pitted sense of anxiety needing only the slightest push to show itself. She'd immediately regretted the decision to bring the boy.

Vetron had every intention of being the sales department's kicker, to kick the ball off. His legs were encased in cylindrical, pipe-like casings that allowed no room to bend at the knee. Normally this wasn't an issue. He had little need to run and kick during the average workday. Only in emergencies would he need to take the stairs, and there'd be no emergencies on Vetron's watch of Vetron & Associates . That was another purpose of his.

His sales department teammates demurred, encouraged Vetron to let someone with more mobility kick, like Nick Claven, who was extremely limber and indicated this to Vetron by kicking his leg up high over his own head. Vetron was unimpressed, though he arguably should have been. Everyone else was, even Janice Debois, who was also very limber and headed the company yoga lessons at 5:30 in the evening on Tuesdays and Thursdays.

Vetron ripped the ball away from the man who'd volunteered to officiate the game, and then he floated it in the air and punted it to the accounting team, despite the fact that it was a kickoff and he was supposed to have kicked the ball to the accounting team from the ground. No one was in position. It had been an egregiously petulant display, that of a spoiled person. Worse than that for Vetron, the ball tumbled forward, no more than fifteen yards, with barely any arc and absolutely no force behind it. This was an obvious consequence of Vetron being virtually unable to lift his legs, and completely unable to bend them. The word "Motherfucker" resounded, in a muffled way, from inside Vetron's helmet. Daryl wondered how well Vetron could see out of his golden visor.

All that could be said of the game that followed was that Vetron failed memorably. He couldn't even disrupt anyone's progress when hurling his metal body at them because all they'd need to do was step aside, for he moved so slowly and with such effort the laws of physics took care of the rest. There was always plenty of time to get out of Vetron's way, and he frequently would only come to a stop by stumbling to the ground, hard and painfully. With great difficulty each time, he labored back up to his feet. The process then began again. By the end, Vetron was as furious as he'd been since changing his name to Vetron. The sales department had won, but Vetron contributed no part of the victory. Indeed, it was in spite of him that they'd bested the accounting department's team, which was actually pretty formidable this year.

Eric Vetron had noticed Vetron's lack of success in the game, as had everyone else, though he'd only been idly paying attention, as was the custom for most in attendance. There was a little more interest than usual, though, given Vetron's presence on the playing field. Eric was drinking a domestic beer from a bottle and nodded a few times in solidarity with his employees lining up against one another. Some of them noticed and returned the gesture. Eric also commented on Vetron—not so much his play as his presence in the office over the past few months. He said he knew Vetron's methods had been extreme, but there was no denying their necessity. Staff members had to be cut, as the market of Vetron and Associate's particular industry retracted due to various unsympathetic global and national economic forces.

Eric Vetron went on, "I think the thing I'm most worried about, in terms of how people and personal interfacing of the future will grow and evolve, is people being too sincere. We've gotten to a 'too sincere' point in time. Novels, too sincere. Television, lots of sincerity, dripping with sincerity. Nudity that's sincere is nudity I don't need. All art is way too comfortable telling us like it is. That's why I've always loved commercials. Nobody actually believes them. They know when we say *Vetron & Associates is the best company to invest in through the mouth of some snappily dressed spokesman and/or spokeswoman*, we're really just saying we want your money. But we're not *saying* it.

We're saying something altogether different, saying one thing and not the other, but meaning the other thing and not the one thing. I want a return to irony, whether it does anything or not. In fact, better for it to do nothing, honestly. Better for it to have nothing to say. Look at Vetron. There's a man with nothing to say. Go on, look, will you?"

Those who were listening to Eric Vetron fell into two camps regarding what he'd said. They either agreed with him unhesitantly or they suspected he was presently battling a pretty severe addiction to controlled substances, which would have explained his general absence around the office likewise. They, too, agreed with him, though, while considering where they might send their resumes at the soonest possible opportunity.

Vetron stared at them from across the field, appearing almost wistful because of his gold visor. There was no emotion there, naturally, but the way the visor tilted, it could have been mistaken for a wistful glance. He was not wistful, though. The gears were at work, turning intensely toward some new mode of thought. He'd been too easy on his colleagues. He'd created this world for himself, for no one else. He wouldn't be embarrassed again.

Vetron heard the noise of a running child padding toward him too late. Nothing could prevent him from being kicked in the face.

Molly shouted, "Stop! No!"

＊

"Everyone can be successful," Daryl said the next day. "I know that's true." He was trying to console Molly, who sat at her desk with folded tissue in her hands. She wasn't crying as much as she had been earlier.

"He's not well," was all she could muster in response. She continued to fold her tissue.

"Try implementing the proper changes," Vetron said, banging from behind Daryl and Molly. They heard his approach and knew he probably meant to speak to them. Vetron's helmet was completely broken. Molly's kid delivered a good, strong kick. The helmet had been a bad helmet, deeply flawed. It was easily cracked down the center. The helmet's weakness had probably always been there, and the boy just provided the necessary force to reveal it. Eventually, the helmet came apart in two pieces.

"I'm so sorry, Vetron. He's never done anything like that. Not that it's OK. I don't mean to imply that it's OK. We have had our troubles with him. We're really hoping things get better soon," Molly said.

"I wish I could say I believe your boy will be alright, in the end. I have learned a few things during my time behind the helmet, and one of them is that absolute candor has its place. Your boy won't ever be normal. He'll always be waiting for the next opportunity to kick someone in the face," Vetron said.

"How could you possibly know that?" Daryl said.

"You learn a lot behind the helmet. As soon as I find a replacement, I'll be back to learning again," Vetron said.

Molly was relieved Vetron hadn't asked her to pay for a new helmet. She knew she probably should have offered to do so, but it wasn't something she was willing to go out of her way to offer. The helmet had been judgmental, constantly judgmental. After Vetron's rudeness and the fact that it had been a weird couple months with him at work, wearing the helmet, she was glad it was gone. She'd prefer it stayed that way, despite how glassy his eyes had gotten.

Daryl couldn't get over the feeling that when Vetron looked at him, especially without the helmet, there was nothing there but pitying disdain. He tried not to take it personally, since that's the way Vetron looked at everyone. Especially without the helmet. He hoped Vetron would get a new helmet soon. He was probably disgusted with Vetron. That's probably why he couldn't wait for Vetron to get a new helmet. He wouldn't have to see his true face anymore.

*

Another meeting was called the following day. Once more, everyone found seating in the conference room. They were asked to silence their phones via Greg, an intern, or more specifically the PowerPoint presentation Greg was operating at the front of the conference room.

Greg looked like a nice kid who didn't really want to be there, working the powerpoint presentation. He looked like he might be rethinking his major, even. Maybe something more labor intensive, like some sort of builder of things.

Vetron entered the room. He nodded at Greg.

The first slide read:

> *I intend to limit the amount of spoken words I use from now on. I'll communicate using text whenever possible. The reason for this is threefold.*

> *1.) To serve you all best, I need more objectivity, and communicating with you personally heightens the risk of feelings of attachment and close relation.*

> *2.) Communication therefore being in fact a hindrance to my job also lessens my personal efficiency. I can get more*

done in a working day if I prevent myself from engaging in collegial banter.

The second seemed a jab at Daryl, Daryl thought, still enjoying the sensation of his muscles flexing involuntarily.

3.) I'll be setting an important example for you all to follow. Fraternizing is to be generally discouraged for the sake of productivity. Please remember this.

And so, the third confirmed it, at least in Daryl's mind. He was stricken with the fear that Vetron was gunning for him. It was stupid, but perhaps, if he were more like Vetron, he could blend in easily, avoid the sorts of entanglements that everyone knew Vetron was on the lookout for. It was stupid. And Vetron's megalomania—now *that* was stupid. Still, though, he was going to avoid calling things stupid out loud. He had to correct his bad habits.

"Was that the end of the meeting?" someone whispered. Vetron waded up to this person, as though walking against a light current in a shallow stream. Standing in front of this person, Vetron pointed to the projection. It was still the one that read, bluntly, *Fraternizing is to be generally discouraged*, etc. The person, gnawing eponychium and looking in the direction Vetron pointed, said, "Oooooh," in a vain attempt at feigning to understand Vetron's intent. Vetron lifted this person and clumsily (because Vetron wasn't particularly strong) threw this person from the conference room.

There was yet another slide. Greg clicked to it after Vetron removed the person who'd spoken. It said, *That's how things will be now.* Everyone applauded, lots of nervous energy sent through the room, anxiety so forceful it almost had a taste, a smell. It smelled like human meat's digestion, Daryl thought. He had watched a documentary about a cannibalistic serial killer in Eastern Europe, and one of the things the documentary noted was that, when you eat human, over time, your body emits a distinct and horrible odor. That was the smell, the collusion of anxious, nauseous feelings. He considered the fact that he'd never eaten anyone, but still he reeked of that odor. They all did. The end of the slide show included the visual of a new logo: a white X outlined in black and a black circle just behind it. This was Vetron the man's logo, presumably, and which he quickly confirmed. "Wherever you see this logo, my logo," Vetron said. "You'll know how to conduct yourself."

That was it. The meeting was now over.

Everyone filed out of the conference room to discover the logo now lined the hallways, repeated over and over. It was drawn in the parking garage, within the demarcation of all the spots, with the exception of those reserved for people with disabilities, whose spots still remained filled with the outline of a person in a wheelchair. But the person in the wheelchair had a malevolent quality to it, despite its being unaltered by Vetron's logo. The logo was in the building's lobby, where personnel from other businesses that occupied the building would see it, as well. No one put up any fuss, though. It was accepted that the logo should be there, everywhere it was.

People were conscious of Vetron's presence at all times. This changed their behavior in peculiar ways, somewhat unexpected ways. There was the effect of the panopticon, obviously, that they felt themselves constantly under surveillance and so made sure to always be properly behaved. Many of them, however, found that they grew to enjoy being in Vetron's favor, living up to his expectations. They had to take satisfaction in something. This is, at least, what a number of the Vetron & Associates unconsciously thought.

Molly had started wearing a helmet at the front desk. She wasn't interested in wearing a full-body Vetron suit, but she did like the helmet. She made it comfortable to wear, filled with cushioning that cradled her head and felt like a pillow. There was no way to make a helmet look nice, so she went with something plain. It was entirely black and utilitarian. She could breathe easily in it. Her head was comfortable inside it, too. She thought she might put a suit on her kid, too, and the helmet. That would prevent him from biting. She figured maybe she and Griff could hold the kid down and fasten padding similar to the kind in her helmet around the boy's hands, too, while they were at it.

Vetron noticed the "Lost Rabbit: is named, though doesn't necessarily answer to, Rebecca" bulletin Daryl had posted in the break room. Vetron analyzed the bulletin closely and computed a reasonable response: immediate removal and a conversation with Daryl regarding appropriate use of the break room announcement board. Vetron tore up the bulletin, making confetti of the colored photo of Rebecca and her unusually mottled fur. Vetron then removed a copy of his logo from his briefcase and thumbtacked it in the place where Daryl's bulletin had been.

Employee Daryl. I need to have a word with you, supervisor to subordinate, Vetron wrote on his notepad for Daryl to read. He was at Daryl's cubicle.

"Oh, Vetron. What's the problem?" Daryl said.

Vetron scribbled.

It is the posting you posted on the announcement board on the wall. That did not pertain to company business. All postings are to in some way relate to company business. Answer in the affirmative if you understand.

Daryl shrugged, slumped in his chair and said he did understand, but added, "I posted that over a month ago, before the rules were put in place. I forgot to take it down."

Unacceptable. We make the rules and your job is to follow them, to the best of your ability. But your ability should be constantly operating at its best. Why bother coming to work if you're unwilling to give anything but? So the best of your ability should be your very best at all times, with no letting down ever. Answer in the affirmative if you understand.

"I'm having a little trouble following, actually, Vetron." Not only was Daryl becoming confused, he was also becoming angry. He had honestly forgotten about the bulletin he posted in the breakroom but he didn't see why it should matter, anyway. It was nice to hope that someone might have seen it and helped him locate his lost Rebecca. It would be a small comfort to have Rebecca returned to him. Why should his life be bereft of the possibility of such a small comfort?

"It doesn't matter if you follow. All that matters is you don't make the same mistake again," Vetron said aloud, affecting an even more monotonal voice than he had in the past.

"I don't think I will. I'm not interested in obeying the rules of a controlling man-robot. You can hope and try for things to be different, but things won't be any different. It won't happen. It's good that it won't. You don't even know what you are anymore, do you? Who are you?"

"I'm Vetron." he said with a strongly bewildered lilt.

"Yeah, but I know there's other stuff in there." Daryl gripped Vetron's metal body. It didn't seem so unyielding in his hands. Vetron didn't seem unyielding at all, suddenly.

"Release me," Vetron said, but he couldn't wrangle from Daryl's grasp and there was one around to help him. What's more, Daryl was much stronger than Vetron, and Vetron's outer shell continued to limit his mobility in every way, including how far his arms could extend outwardly. He was at Daryl's mercy.

Daryl found the spot where Vetron's metal shell was bolted closed. He pulled hard at the seams and nothing happened at first, but after a couple of seconds of this, Daryl heard the sound of nuts springing from their fixtures and falling off. He pulled the body apart, and there, beneath the shell, was Vetron's human form. Vetron wore red underwear and possessed the paunch of a middle-aged man.

Daryl turned from Vetron. He left the office and the building.

Outside, he thought he saw Rebecca.

He went running in the direction he thought he saw her go.

No one saw much of Daryl after that.

acknowledgements

There are so many people who are owed much praise for the existence of this book I fear excluding even one of them. I'll start with my wife, Michelle, and our daughter, Keira, both of whom energize me to do most everything I do, and certainly this book is one example of said energies. *How the Moon Works* simply would not exist in its present form without them. I should likewise mention Michael and Carolyn Rowan, my parents, and sister, Allison Miller, and brother, Sean Stone. I would not exist in my present form without you.

This book is a labor of love that has been in progress for well over a decade now, going all the way back to when I was twenty-something, starry-eyed know-it-all. Over that period, I received much help and feedback from Alex Fernandez (who, among other things, gave me the idea for the title of the titular short story), Jamie Ferguson, Lucy Boone, Jon Mau (all of them my peerless reviewers), and Jim Swakow (please blame Jim for anything about this collection you don't like).

Many thanks to James Tadd Adcox, Jon Trobaugh, Meghan Lamb, Lyndee Yamshon and Rose Pacult, all of whom provided helpful notes at various points in this manuscript's development.

I would be remiss not to mention Fusion Academy Los Angeles and the many students, administrators, and faculty who've helped me (and so too this book) along the way. Mitch Carver, in particular, is owed an extra effusive shout out. Thanks, Mitch!

Without question, I owe very much (from design, to editorial insights, to enduring my non-stop questions) to Andrew Keating of Cobalt Press.

notes

Pieces in this collection originally appeared, in slightly altered form, in the following publications:

"No Me Say It" in *Timber Journal*
"Eyesore of a Thing" in *Toad: the Journal*
"Not the Actions of a Hero Who Must Be Nice" originally
  published as "Must Be, No Reason" in *BULL*
"Enthusiasm for the Final Climactic Showdown" in *The Bicycle
  Review*
"The Walk-in-Their-Footsteps Historical Footsteps Museum" in
  Untoward Magazine
"Watch Him Squeeze Stuff" in *Another Chicago Magazine*

about the author

Matt Rowan lives in Los Angeles with his wife and daughter. He edits *Untoward* and is author of the short story collections *Big Venerable* and *Why God Why*. He's hard at work on multiple novels and very hopeful one of them will finally cooperate and be completed soon.

CPSIA information can be obtained
at www.ICGtesting.com
Printed in the USA
BVHW031731261021
619923BV00007B/156

9 781941 462249